Books by Tom Hoffman

Bartholomew the Adventurer • The Eleventh Ring
Bartholomew the Adventurer • The Thirteenth Monk
Bartholomew the Adventurer • The Seventh Medallion

•••

Orville Mouse and the Puzzle of the Clockwork Glowbirds
Orville Mouse and the Puzzle of the Shattered Abacus
Orville Mouse and the Puzzle of the Capricious Shadows
Orville Mouse and the Puzzle of the Last Metaphonium
Orville Mouse and the Puzzle of the Sagacious Sapling

•••

The Translucent Boy and the Girl Who Saw Him
The Translucent Boy and the Cat Who Ran Out of Time
The Translucent Boy and the Girl Who Dreamed She Could Fly
The Translucent Boy and the Man Who Walked to the Moon
The Translucent Boy and the Children of Ice

•••

The Comet Kid Chronicles • Under the Blue Comet
The Comet Kid Chronicles • The Unfocused Man
The Comet Kid Chronicles • The Sinister Sorcerer

•••

The Ghost Ring • Welcome to Wilder House
The Ghost Ring • Shadows of Caligo Falls
The Ghost Ring • The Haunting of Caligo Farm

•••

Miss Bristol Rents a Room

Miss Bristol
RENTS A ROOM

TOM HOFFMAN

Cover design by Tom Hoffman Graphic Design
Anchorage, Alaska

Tom Hoffman
Visit my website at thoffmanak.wordpress.com
Email: OrvilleMouse@gmail.com

Printed in the United States of America

First Printing: 2025
ISBN 979-8-9884059-8-6

For my amazing wife Alexis,
who has put up with my crazy
for over fifty years.
Love you always.

"We must not allow the clock and the calendar to blind us to the fact that each moment of life is a miracle and mystery."

H.G. Wells

**“Everything we call real
is made of things that cannot
be regarded as real.”**

Niels Bohr

Miss Bristol
RENTS A ROOM

Chapter 1

"When everything is lost, and all seems darkness, then comes the new life and all that is needed."
—Joseph Campbell

Miss Bristol

Miss Bristol entered this world on September 20, 2025, arriving unexpectedly just before noon near the corner of Bogart and Moore Streets in Brooklyn, New York. More unexpected than her arrival, however, was the unusual nature of her wardrobe—elegant attire that would have been haute couture for a young woman of means strolling down Fifth Avenue in 1910, during the waning years of what Mark Twain so famously called the Gilded Age. Although Miss Bristol's clothing was undeniably elegant, the particular circumstances of her arrival were not.

MISS BRISTOL RENTS A ROOM

Young Miss Bristol staggered out of a darkened alleyway like the proverbial drunken sailor, clearly impaired by some unknown agent, her delicately embroidered travel bag tumbling to the sidewalk with a soft thud as she pressed both hands to her head, leaning over, fearing she might faint, or vomit, or both. A searing headache was blurring her vision, Miss Bristol feeling as if her skull was being crushed by some devilishly conceived medieval iron vise. She fell to her knees, collapsing with a low moan onto her soft woolen carpet bag, pressing her face against it, her body in shock, her mind numb. She lay there for almost twenty minutes, her headache eventually diminishing, her pounding heart gradually slowing to a more measured rate.

A few passersby gave her the odd look, a perfunctory glance at her flaming bright orange hair, but nothing more substantial.

She tried to focus, taking in her surroundings: the tall brick buildings, the strange metal and glass vehicles rolling past on the wide smooth city street. It was all quite unfamiliar, but she had no idea if what she was seeing was new or old, having no memories to compare it to. She looked down at her clothes: a pale blue fitted jacket cinched neatly at the waist, navy velvet lapels, a crisp white blouse with a high laced collar, and a long gored skirt almost concealing her highly polished buttoned boots. She had a folded newspaper gripped tightly in her right hand. She sat up, looked around, then unfolded the newspaper, studying the front page, her vision still slightly blurred.

New York Tribune September 12, 1910

Airships Dazzle Long Island Spectators!

Wright Flyers Perform Stunts in Weekend Exhibition

She had no idea what the headline meant, but now she knew the year was 1910. She gingerly got to her feet, trying to steady herself, a sudden flood of heat rushing up through her body. She leaned over, afraid she might faint again, then sat down. This was unbearable, nightmarish. Who was she? Where was she? Was this her home? Did she have a home? The world surrounding her was so strangely unfamiliar, so foreign to her. She must be dreaming; what else could it be?

She closed her eyes, willing herself to awaken. When she opened them again, nothing had changed. She tried again, gritting her teeth this time, again failing to awaken. A dark thought came to her. It was a fit of apoplexy, a sudden seizure which had caused her loss of memory. She was ill, a brain disorder of some kind. Or worse, maybe she was dead. If she was dead, why was she not in heaven? Where were the angels?

She reached up, pulling a long jeweled pin from her orange hair, jabbing it sharply into her finger. There was pain and there was a drop of blood. This definitively resolved two of her most pressing concerns: she was not dead and she was not dreaming. How did she know she had a jeweled pin in her hair?

She ran her hand across the embroidered travel bag, feeling its texture, trying to remember where it came from, if it even belonged to her. She pulled it onto her lap, unhooking the rounded brass clasp, opening it, examining the contents: a chemise, stockings, a garter belt, a pale blue silk skirt, a petticoat. There was a purple velvet bag holding a hairbrush, three combs, face powder, Daggett & Ramsdell vanishing cream, several hair tonics, Melba rouge, and a small red leather purse holding ten gold coins. At least she had money, that was important. One of the bottles of hair tonic proudly stated that the company had been established in 1889. That made sense, since the year was 1910. She searched the bag for any identifying documents, something with her name on it; an envelope, a calling card, but found nothing.

Her faintness had passed, her headache much diminished. She got to her feet, her travel bag in one hand, stepping over to a nearby green metal bench and taking a seat, resting the carpet bag on her lap. She watched two scruffy-looking teenage boys walk past wearing blue denim trousers with holes in the knees, undershirts with words and symbols printed on them, and oddly shaped colorful shoes. One of the boys glanced back at her, calling out, "Nice hair, freak." They both laughed as they walked away.

Why had they said that? Why would they call her a freak? Why were they laughing at her? It seemed to be an unusually cruel thing to say to a person they didn't even know. She leaned forward, covering her face with both hands, trying to think. A dreadful thought occurred to her. She had no idea what her face looked like. Maybe she had a hideously freakish mis-shapen face, maybe that's what they were laughing about. This was a most disturbing thought. She needed to look in a mirror.

She opened her travel bag, rummaging through the bag of toiletries, finding a small mirror, holding it in front of her, desperately afraid of what she might see. She gazed at her reflection. It was not freakish, she was almost attractive looking, some might call her pretty, with lovely bright orange hair, and sparkling orange eyes. This was an immense relief to her. She closed the mirror, returning it to the velvet bag. Her thoughts were clearer now, not as jumbled.

If it were a fit of apoplexy which had caused her to lose her memory, perhaps there was someone nearby who knew her, someone who would recognize her, a neighbor perhaps, someone who would be kind enough to help her.

She glanced down the street, studying the shops, noting the refuse on the sidewalks: old newspapers, wrappers, a smashed bottle, an old shirt. This was uncalled for, someone should clean it up. Under normal circumstances she would most certainly write a letter to the newspaper's editor regarding the unsightly refuse, but these were far from normal circumstances. When she thought about it, she had no idea what normal circumstances would be.

She gripped her travel bag and stood up, spotting a shop down the street with a dozen people seated outside at small tables—a cafe perhaps. Maybe there was someone she knew there, someone who would recognize her.

As she walked toward the cafe, she spotted an elderly woman sitting on a green bench facing the street, more than likely waiting for a trolley. She approached the woman, attempting a pleasant, disarming smile; a polite but friendly demeanor.

"Excuse me, madam. I know this is a most curious

question, but I can't seem to remember who I am. I wonder if perhaps you have seen me here before? Do you happen to recognize me?"

The woman looked up at her, shaking her head, averting her eyes, looking away.

Miss Bristol sighed, realizing that such a course of action would inevitably prove unsuccessful. Clearly there were far too many people in this city for her to chance upon someone she knew. She stopped short, a thought occurring to her. Was she actually in New York City, the same city as the newspaper she had been holding, or was she in another city? Perhaps that was why it felt so foreign to her.

She looked across the street, noticing a covered stand displaying racks of newspapers and magazines. She would most certainly find some answers there.

She crossed the street, approaching the newspaper stand, eyeing the rather disheveled-looking vendor leaning back in a wooden chair, an unlit cigar in his mouth, his clothes wrinkled, his hair in need of a good brushing. She studied the newspapers, noting they were from a variety of cities, not just New York.

"Pardon me sir, can you tell me if you sell a local newspaper?"

He pointed to a stack of papers in front of her. "The New York Times, that local enough?" He gave a raucous laugh.

She studied the paper closely, making no response to his laugh. It was indeed the New York Times, proving conclusively that she was in New York. This was good news. Her insides twisted, however, when she read the date on the paper—September 20, 2025. This was most concerning, and more than upsetting. She had been so certain the year was 1910.

She pointed to the stack of newspapers. "Would this be today's newspaper, sir?"

"It ain't yesterday's and it ain't tomorrow's." He gave the same raucous laugh, Miss Bristol finding it somewhat annoying.

"Thank you, sir."

He studied her face, then her clothes, taking the cigar from his mouth.

"You some kind of actress? On Broadway?"

Miss Bristol nodded politely, no idea why he would ask such a thing, but impulsively answered, "Yes, an actress, on Broadway." Why had she said that? She had no memories of being an actress, clearly something she would have remembered.

"That new Gilded Age show? The wife and I are going next week. Cost a freaking fortune but we go see a play on her birthday every year. Good place to take a nap, no offense." He laughed again.

"Yes, the Gilded Age show."

"Thought so. Your outfit kinda gave it away." He laughed, but this time it seemed to be a genuine laugh.

Miss Bristol smiled in return. "Quite so."

"You doin' okay? You're looking a little rough, young lady. Do a little celebrating last night?"

She smiled again. "I'm quite fine, thank you." She left without buying a paper, trying to make sense of what she had just seen. It would appear she was living in the year 2025. If this was so, why was she holding a newspaper from 1910? One solution to this dilemma might be that she was indeed an actress, that she actually was in the show about the Gilded Age, and perhaps the newspaper was a prop from the play.

She closed her eyes for a moment. It was truly unbearable not knowing who she was. Where should she go? Where would she sleep? Did she have a home here? Perhaps she should seek out a doctor to determine if it was a sudden seizure which had caused her memory loss. She realized she was famished, no idea when her last meal had been. Or where it had been.

She looked down the street at the cafe with the outside tables, a dozen people seated at them, chatting, laughing, eating and drinking, all of them knowing who they were, where they were, and why they were there.

She continued down the street, approaching the cafe, reading the colorful sign that ran across the front of the building.

Mama Rosa's Pizza

The Best in Brooklyn, Maybe the World

Miss Bristol frowned, having no idea what pizza was, or who Mama Rosa was. The people dining there seemed to be enjoying their meal, however, so it must be a reputable cafe. She strolled past the tables, several diners glancing up at her curiously as she passed them, then stepped through the front door, taking her place in line. There were four people in front of her, Miss Bristol reading the colorful menu displayed on the wall behind the counter, trying to make sense of it. It would seem there were a great many varieties of pizza to choose from, but she had no idea which one to purchase, whether it should be a round or a triangular-shaped one. Was there a difference between them? She would ask the clerk for his recommendation, removing from her the burden of choice.

When it was her turn, she stepped up to the counter, six people now in line behind her.

"Good afternoon, sir. Would you be so kind as to offer me your recommendation regarding the various varieties of pizza? I am quite unfamiliar with–"

"What do you want? What kind of pizza?"

"What kind would you recommend, sir?"

The man turned and shouted, "One slice of pepperoni!"

Twenty seconds later he set down a paper plate holding a large triangular slice of pizza.

"Four bucks."

Miss Bristol nodded with a quizzical smile, saying, "Bucks?"

"Four dollars."

She reached into her travel bag, pulling out the small red purse, removing one of the gold coins, placing it on the counter.

The clerk glared at her, clearly annoyed. "Cash or plastic. We got a line here, let's move it along."

"I'm afraid I am unfamiliar with plastic, sir. Will this coin not suffice?"

He mumbled something darkly under his breath, then slid the pizza toward her. "This is your lucky day, girl. I'm feeling generous. Take the slice and go, we don't got time for your shenanigans."

Miss Bristol retrieved her coin, turning to leave. As she was opening the door, she heard the clerk say to no one in particular, "That girl needs help."

Her interaction with the clerk had proven most upsetting to Miss Bristol. If this was her home, if this was where she lived, why did she not know what plastic was? Why was she unfamiliar with pizza, clearly a popular food of the day? She noticed several diners staring at her curiously, which she found to be most disconcerting. She decided to exude an aura of confidence, acting as if she was quite familiar with her surroundings.

She spotted an empty table, pulling out a chair and sitting down, casually setting the plate of pizza in front of her. She scanned the table for silverware, but found none. This was quite baffling—why would a reputable cafe not provide silverware? As unobtrusively as she was able, she stole quick glances at the other diners, watching how they ate their pizza. They were not using silverware, but instead, they were folding the slice of pizza in half lengthwise, and eating it with their bare hands. She grimaced, a look of distaste crossing her face. She looked down at her pizza, deciding whether or not to fold it and eat it with her hands. Perhaps she should leave. Her indecision was interrupted by a friendly voice.

"Excuse me, miss. Would you mind terribly if I sat at your table? The other tables are quite full."

She looked up, eyeing the white-haired old man wearing a crisp gray suit and tie, a folded handkerchief peeking neatly out of his breast pocket.

"Of course, sir. I will confess I could use some friendly company."

"Wonderful, I thank you. I must say, it has been many years since I dined with a lovely young lady such as yourself."

He pulled out a chair and took a seat, smiling at Miss Bristol. "I could not help but notice you were uncertain about what kind of pizza to get?"

"Yes, quite uncertain. I must confess, this is the first time I have had pizza."

The man raised his eyebrows imperceptibly.

Miss Bristol corrected herself. "That is to say, sir, I have never had pizza at this particular cafe before. There are so many varieties here to choose from that I was momentarily baffled."

He gave an understanding nod. "Of course, it can be quite daunting, deciding which kind to order, with so many toppings, and an almost infinite variety of combinations to choose from. I find myself at times uncertain which toppings I should like to select."

Miss Bristol decided she liked this old man. He was kind, considerate of others. She watched as he folded his pizza in half, taking a bite. "Mmm, delicious as always. I have my lunch here every day at noon, like clockwork. Excellent pizza."

Miss Bristol smiled, following his lead, folding her

pizza in half. When in Rome, do as the Romans do. She blinked. She had no idea who the Romans were or what they did.

Chapter 2

"That's how you do it, young lady, now you're eating pizza like a true New Yorker." He laughed.

Miss Bristol liked his laugh, it was the laugh of someone she could trust. "I shall confess that I am quite new to the city, and quite disoriented."

"You have just arrived in the city? I see you are carrying a travel bag?"

"Yes, I just arrived today."

"Your outfit is quite charming, from a different era, most becoming."

"I'm an actress, on Broadway, that show about the Gilded Age." She felt some guilt in misleading him, but she didn't know what else to say, how to explain away her clothing.

"I should have guessed it. How marvelous to meet such a gifted person."

"I don't have anywhere to stay yet. It's all quite confusing."

The old man rubbed his chin. "Would you mind if

an old man gave you a little advice about New York?"

"Of course, I would be most grateful, sir."

"First things first, rent a room. That is my advice. Do not stay in a hotel, they are exorbitantly expensive, well beyond the means of most visitors. Find a cozy, comfortable room to rent in a nice neighborhood, far less expensive than a hotel and far more relaxing."

"Shall I search for rooms-to-let in a local newspaper?"

The man paused, then said, "I suspect there is no need for that now, as I may have a ready solution for you, young lady. As luck would have it, on the way here I passed a row house with a room-for-rent sign in the front window. It's in a lovely neighborhood, and quite close by. That might be a good place to start. Walk two blocks down Moore Street in that direction, take a right on Bogart, then a left on Thames. You can't miss it."

"Thank you so much, you have been more than kind."

"You're quite welcome, miss. I'm here every day at noon, if you need any more of my grandfatherly advice."

"I do have several questions I should like to ask, if you have time?"

"Of course."

"The clerk here said they only take plastic, not gold coins. I'm afraid I am quite unfamiliar with plastic."

"I see. What he is referring to are small plastic cards like this one, called credit cards." He pulled a wallet from his pocket, showing her a small stack of rectangular credit cards. "It is a convenient way to exchange funds without the burden of carrying cash or coins on your person."

"Do I give the card to the clerk as payment? How do I get another credit card?"

"You only need one. You hand your card to the clerk, and he scans it with a machine that reads the card and transfers the cost of the pizza from your account to the pizza shop's account, then he hands the card back to you. At the end of every month you pay the credit card company all the money you spent during that month. It's quite convenient once you learn how to use it."

"How does the machine know where to send the money?"

"An excellent question, but one with a rather complex answer. There is a global electronic network called the internet, a little like the telephone system of the old days, but a thousand times faster and far more complex, spanning the entire globe. I could send money to France if I wanted to, and it would be there in less than a second."

"How astonishing, and completely baffling. It is quite miraculous."

"It is indeed, miss. I scarcely understand it myself. It might do you well to find a book about computers and the internet, read up on them."

"I shall do exactly that, sir. I have one last question regarding renting a room."

"I shall do my best to answer it."

"How shall I pay for a room if I don't have plastic?"

"Did I hear you say you had a gold coin?"

"Yes, I have two hundred dollars worth of gold coins, but the clerk would not accept them as payment."

"May I see one of them?"

Miss Bristol opened her small red purse, handing one of the gold coins to the old man. He studied it closely, looking up at Miss Bristol curiously, then back at the coin, turning it over slowly in his hand.

"This is a twenty dollar gold coin, a Double Eagle, from 1910, in near uncirculated condition."

Miss Bristol nodded. "It is indeed, sir. How much do you think it shall cost to rent a room for one month? Would it be more than twenty dollars?"

"Do you have any idea the value of this coin, or the

current value of gold? I think you shall be pleasantly surprised."

Miss Bristol shook her head. "Is it not twenty dollars, as it clearly states on the coin?"

"It is not. Gold is currently selling at over three thousand dollars an ounce. This coin weighs approximately one ounce, and has the added value of being a rare coin in near uncirculated condition."

"Three thousand dollars for an ounce of gold? Are you certain of this? It sounds quite preposterous."

"I am certain. How many coins do you have?"

"I have ten similar coins."

"I should like to assist you, young lady. We must go to a coin shop and sell two of your coins. Dealers can be quite unscrupulous at times, so it would be best if I went there with you and sold the coins for you. Is that acceptable?"

"I would more than welcome your help, sir, as I know nothing of such things."

When they had finished lunch, Miss Bristol and the old man walked three blocks to a dilapidated old shop with wrought iron bars over the windows, the wooden sign above it reading *Frankie's Cash & Coin Shop*.

They stepped inside, the man behind the counter giving the old man a friendly greeting. "Nice to see you again, sir. Are you buying or selling?"

"This time I am selling. I have two near uncirculated Double Eagles from 1910. Nicest ones I've seen in a long time. Ungraded, too." He set the two gold coins down gently on a rectangular velvet pad.

The man slipped on a white cotton glove, picking up one of the coins, studying it closely under a magnifying glass, then examined the second coin. "You're right, these are nice, and both Denver mints. I'll give you three thousand each, cash."

"I was thinking thirty-five hundred—as you said, they are Denver mints."

"You're killin' me. Thirty-two each, final offer."

"Done."

Ten minutes later a stunned Miss Bristol was tucking a thick wad of bills into her travel bag. She impulsively reached out, taking the old man's hand. "How can I ever thank you for your kindness, sir? This is a gift from heaven above. I could never have done this without your help. I don't even know your name."

"Everyone calls me Ben. Perhaps we could have lunch again sometime, if you happen to be at Mama Rosa's at noon?"

"It would please me no end. I will see you again, it is a promise I shall keep."

"Thames Street is one block down that way. Turn right on Thames, the room for rent is about half a block down."

Miss Bristol took her leave, waving her good bye, heading toward Thames Street. As she strolled down the street, eyeing the tidy brick row houses, she smiled. Ben was right, this was a nice neighborhood. It felt safe—there were children playing outside, laughing, riding their bicycles, bouncing a ball.

She spotted the room-for-rent sign in the front window of a well-kept row house, a string of ten numbers written on the sign. She had no idea what the numbers were for.

Walking up the wrought iron steps to the front door, she knocked on it. When there was no answer, she knocked again, louder. A minute later the door cracked open, a middle-aged woman peering out at her, studying her. "May I help you?"

"I am inquiring about the room you have for rent. A good friend of mine directed me to your home."

The woman stared at her, looking at her clothes. "Why didn't you call first? Phone number is right there." She pointed to the string of numbers on the sign.

"I'm afraid I don't have a telephone."

"A young woman without a phone? That's new. Why are you dressed like that?"

Miss Bristol had prepared her answer. "I am an

actress on Broadway, that new show about the Gilded Age."

"That explains it. I thought you might be, how can I say it, happily living in a world no one else can see?" She laughed, the door swinging open, the woman motioning for her to enter.

Miss Bristol had a warm feeling the moment she entered the house. There was something about it, something deeply comforting, and the woman renting the room seemed very nice, trustworthy. "This is a lovely home."

"Thank you. We try to keep it in good repair, but what with the price of things these days it's hard to keep up with just one salary. Harlan and I decided it was time to rent out the spare room on the third floor. It's small, but it's clean and comfortable. You have your own bathroom, a small kitchenette with a microwave, a coffee maker, mini-fridge, and a small television."

Miss Bristol nodded, having no idea what a microwave, mini-fridge, or a television was.

"No parties allowed. Do you have a boyfriend?"

Miss Bristol shook her head. "I just arrived here in New York. I have no boyfriend, and there will be no parties and no visitors, I can assure you of that."

"It's a thousand dollars a month, and that's a

bargain. If you're over three days late with the rent, you're out. No excuses."

Miss Bristol blinked when she heard the cost of renting a room for one month was a thousand dollars. She had been expecting twenty or thirty dollars a month at the most. Why had she been expecting that? On the other hand, she currently had over six thousand dollars in her travel bag, plus eight more gold coins.

She said, "That sounds quite acceptable. May I see the room?"

"Follow me."

They headed up the stairs to the third floor, walking down a short hallway, the woman opening the door to the room, motioning for Miss Bristol to enter. It took Miss Bristol less than a minute to make up her mind. "This is quite suitable. I will take it. Would you mind showing me how to operate this machine?" She pointed to the microwave.

"Of course, they can be tricky, they're all different. It's annoying."

"And what is that small cabinet for?"

"The mini-fridge? It's a refrigerator."

"There is already ice in it?"

The woman gave her a puzzled look. "It has an icemaker, if that's what you mean."

It was Miss Bristol's turn to be confused, but she said, "Yes, I was curious if it had an ice-maker in it."

"It does." The woman was giving Miss Bristol an odd look.

"I would like to pay for three months of rent in advance, if that is acceptable."

The woman gave her another quizzical look. "That's three thousand dollars."

"Yes, quite correct." Miss Bristol reached into her travel bag, pulling out the wad of cash, counting out three thousand dollars in hundred dollar bills, holding them out to the woman.

"Why do you have so much cash? You're not a drug dealer are you?"

Miss Bristol again looked puzzled. "Are you asking if I am a pharmacist?"

The woman's expression darkened. "I'm asking why you have so much cash."

"I just sold something quite valuable."

"What, like a car?"

Miss Bristol thought it best not to mention the gold coins in her travel bag. "Yes, a car. I just sold a car."

"Wise move, you won't need one in the city, take a bus or a rideshare."

"I shall most certainly be taking the trolley."

The woman laughed. "I love it, you sound like you

just stepped out of the Gilded Age. Take the trolley, hilarious. I'll have to tell Harlan that one. Maybe we'll go see your show."

"Thank you." Miss Bristol laughed in turn, uncertain why her comment had amused the woman so much.

"You can bring in your belongings whenever you want."

Miss Bristol's mind was spinning, searching for an explanation as to why she had no belongings to bring in. "Sadly, all my personal belongings were packed in a steamer trunk, but it has been misplaced in transit. All I have is this travel bag."

"What's your name, dear?"

Startling Miss Bristol beyond measure, the words fell out of her mouth, as though she had said them a thousand times before. "I am Miss Bristol."

"It's nice to meet you, Miss Bristol. I am Mrs. Wiggins, and my husband is Harlan. He's out of town right now on a case, interviewing witnesses. He's a police detective with NYPD." She appeared to be assessing Miss Bristol's reaction to this new information.

Miss Bristol nodded. "A noble profession indeed."

Miss Bristol heard the front door slam shut, someone calling out, "I'm home!"

Mrs. Wiggins smiled. "It's Silas, he always slams the front door when he gets home from school. He says it's his signature entrance into the house."

"I should like to meet him."

"Of course."

They headed downstairs to the living room, a teenage boy sitting on the couch, his eyes on a wide rectangular screen of moving images, the sound of gunfire and explosions filling the room.

"Silas, game off, you just got home and we have company. This is Miss Bristol, she's going to be renting the spare bedroom on the third floor."

Silas tapped a button and the raucous sounds stopped, Miss Bristol unable to take her eyes off the moving images of horrifying creatures on the screen. "Good heavens, what is that?"

Silas said, "Zombie Apocalypse 4. Are you a gamer?"

"This is a game?"

"Brand new, super fun. What's with your clothes?"

Mrs. Wiggins frowned. "Mind your manners. She's an actress, in the new play about the Gilded Age."

"What's the Gilded Age?"

Mrs. Wiggins gave a sigh. "It was during the late 1800s and early 1900s. People dressed like this, it was all quite elegant."

"Why do you have orange eyes? Are you wearing colored contacts?"

Miss Bristol nodded. "Yes, colored contacts, for the play."

Mrs. Wiggins gave Miss Bristol a sideways glance but said nothing.

"Cool. You want to try playing the game?"

"Is it difficult? I don't understand what you're doing." She turned to Mrs. Wiggins. "Would it be all right with you if Silas showed me how to play his game?"

"Sure, I'll leave you to it."

Silas said, "It's easy, I'll show you. Sit here." He moved over, handing the controller to Miss Bristol. "Push this to make him walk or run and change directions. Push this to make him shoot."

Twenty minutes later Miss Bristol was laughing. "I blasted him, just as you suggested!"

"Nice one, now try blasting the zombies, they're a lot harder to kill, and they move fast. Use the shotgun, that works best."

"What is a zombie?"

"The living dead, reanimated corpses."

"That sounds quite dreadful."

"I know. It's totally awesome, right?"

Half an hour later Mrs. Wiggins returned. “Okay, game time is over. Silas, you have homework?”

“I have some, but I did most of it at school.”

“How did your math test go?”

“Sorry, I only got an A on it. Is that okay?”

“Don’t be a smart aleck.”

Silas gave an exaggerated eye roll. “No one says smart aleck anymore. No one even knows what it means.”

Mrs. Wiggins turned to Miss Bristol. “Could we speak in the kitchen? I have a few more things to tell you about the room.”

“Of course.”

They stepped into the kitchen, Mrs. Wiggins motioning for Miss Bristol to take a seat.

“You seem like a good person, Miss Bristol, but to be quite honest, I feel as though there is something you’re not telling us.” Her face softened. “I have to ask, are you in any kind of trouble? Running away from a boyfriend, a husband? You wouldn’t be the first to do that, and I want you to know you are safe here.”

“It is kind of you to ask, Mrs. Wiggins, but no, I am not running away from anyone. I am quite lost in the city though. It’s far bigger than I had imagined.”

“You say your belongings were lost in shipping?”

"I have a spare outfit in my travel bag, but the garments are quite old-fashioned, similar to the clothes I am wearing."

Mrs. Wiggins nodded, pursing her lips. "I see. I'll tell you what, you're about the same size as Anna, you can borrow some of her clothes until you get some new ones. How does that sound?"

"Anna will not mind?"

"No, it would please her greatly, I'm certain of it."

A completely unexpected wave of profound sadness rolled through Miss Bristol. "Anna is your daughter?"

"Yes, we had two children. You met Silas, but our dear Anna passed on a year ago. She was just about your age. She was hit by a car, a drunk driver." Mrs. Wiggins' eyes instantly welled up.

"I am so sorry, I can only imagine the depth of your grief."

"I haven't touched her room since she left us; I don't have the heart to move her things out. I know she would have loved to lend you some of her clothes; she was such a kind-hearted soul. She loved her clothes, always bringing home some new outfit, modeling it for us, making us laugh."

"I think if I had known her we would have been good friends."

"I'm certain of it. Let's go upstairs and find you some more suitable clothes."

Chapter 3

Mrs. Wiggins led the way up the stairs to the second floor, silently opening the door to Anna's room. They stepped into the room, Miss Bristol eyeing the posters, colorful decorations, flowers, cluttered bookshelves, and a collage of photographs on the wall. She walked over to the photos, studying them. She had never seen colored photographs before, and the images were so sharp and clear. She decided not to comment on this, attempting to appear familiar with such things. She pointed to the image of a smiling teenage girl. "Is this your Anna?"

"Yes, she was beautiful, radiant. She lit up the room."

"She is quite lovely. Are these her friends?"

"They are. She had so many friends. She would have friends over after school almost every day, and we welcomed them. It was chaos, but I liked it. I liked hearing them laugh. My childhood was not filled with laughter." She glanced at Miss Bristol. "I'm sorry, I don't know what made me say that."

"I understand." Miss Bristol walked over to the desk, studying the framed photo of a teenage boy. "Was this also a friend of hers?"

"Her boyfriend. He was with her when it happened. We don't see him anymore. It was too much for him. He couldn't face us; I don't think he knew what to say. It changed him. Silas said he's having a hard time in school, acting out, getting in trouble. I feel so sorry for him."

Miss Bristol nodded. "It is sad to see such things."

Mrs. Wiggins opened the closet doors, Miss Bristol eyeing the dozens of pants, blouses, skirts, and hoodies hanging in the closet, six shelves on one end filled with stacks of neatly folded cotton shirts. "I'll leave you here, you can try things on, see how they fit, see how you like them. Take whatever clothes you like."

"Thank you, Mrs. Wiggins, you have been more than kind. I will confess I have received more than a few curious glances walking about in my Gilded Age costume."

Mrs. Wiggins laughed. "I imagine so. Take your time, dear."

After Mrs. Wiggins left the room, Miss Bristol returned to the collage of photos, carefully studying the clothes worn by Anna and her friends. Many of them wore the close-fitting blue trousers and short-sleeved shirts, some loose and some tight, only two of the girls wearing skirts. Miss Bristol frowned when she saw them, the skirts being scandalously short, quite inappropriate for a proper young lady. All in all, the clothes they wore left nothing to the imagination regarding their figures. She stepped over to the closet, taking out a pair of the blue pants, studying the label. They were called jeans.

Ten minutes later she was standing in front of a full-length mirror wearing her jeans and a purple short-sleeved cotton shirt with an indecipherable symbol on the front. She sighed. Mrs. Wiggins was more than kind, but it was embarrassing to see herself dressed in such clothing. She was wearing pants, like a man, and worse than that, pants that showed off her figure for all the world to see. She walked back over to the photo collage, studying it again. She did look like the girls in the photographs, but she still couldn't get over the fact that she was wearing men's trousers. She gave a sigh. When in Rome, do as the Romans do. She walked back to the closet, picking out two more pairs of jeans and four cotton shirts.

When she was done, she gathered up the clothes and went upstairs to her room, hanging the clothes in her closet, taking a seat on the bed, her eyes on the embroidered travel bag.

She had eight gold coins left—about twenty-five thousand dollars—enough to pay for two years of rent. Despite her current abundance of wealth, she knew her money wouldn't last forever—she'd have to pay for new clothes, food, trolley fare. She stopped herself. There were no trolleys; they had buses, subways, and rideshare cars. She would need to find work, but she had no skills—at least no memory of any skills she may have had before she found herself in the alleyway. It was encouraging that she was making new memories, not forgetting the events which had occurred since her arrival.

She liked her room. It was cozy, comforting. She would thank Ben for his kind advice the next time she saw him. She was lucky to find a good-hearted landlord like Mrs. Wiggins. She suspected Mrs. Wiggins knew she was not an actress, but was not one to pry into her personal affairs. When the time was right, she would tell Mrs. Wiggins everything, about her loss of memory. Unfortunately, she had no idea why she was wearing clothes from the Gilded Age.

Miss Bristol headed downstairs, stepping into the kitchen. Mrs. Wiggins was standing at the stove while Silas sat at the table doing his homework.

"Hello." She looked at them nervously, awaiting their comments on her new wardrobe, hoping they would not laugh.

Silas looked up from his homework. "Whoa, you look totally hot."

Mrs. Wiggins glared at him. "Mind your manners, young man."

"Just thought she'd want to know."

Mrs. Wiggins shook her head. "Not appropriate, Silas."

"Sorry."

Miss Bristol said, "I don't look like a man?"

Silas burst out laughing. "What? Why would you even say that?"

"I'm not used to wearing such clothes as these. I am used to wearing long skirts, not men's trousers." How did she know she always wore long skirts? It was so confusing.

Mrs. Wiggins said, "You look wonderful, Miss Bristol. Anna would be jealous of your beautiful orange hair. You are a lovely young woman."

Silas's grin vanished when his mom mentioned Anna.

Miss Bristol said, "Is there anything I can do to help with dinner? I shall pay for my meals, of course."

"You can help set the table for dinner; plates and

silverware. Don't worry about meals, Miss Bristol. I forgot to mention it, but your rent covers meals. You'll eat dinner with us."

"You're quite certain?"

"Plates are in the cupboard, silverware in that drawer."

They had a lovely dinner, Miss Bristol almost buoyant. For an hour or so, all was right with the world, she didn't have to worry about who she was or where she was, or why she was. This was enough, she was here. Silas was talking about a new app on his phone, whatever that was, when she had an unexpected thought.

When Ben had asked her about the value of the gold coin, she had said it was worth twenty dollars, but the actual value proved to be over three thousand dollars. Why had she assumed it was worth only twenty dollars? Why had she not known the current value of gold?

"Is there a library nearby where I could research something?"

Silas said, "Use your phone."

"I don't have a phone. I was hoping if there was a—"

"What are you trying to find out?"

"I was curious about some gold coins I saw in a

shop. The clerk said they were twenty dollar gold coins, but they were worth far more than that now. I was curious as to when they would have been worth twenty dollars."

Silas tapped on his phone, studying it. "In 1910, gold was about twenty dollars an ounce, and a twenty dollar gold piece weighed about one ounce, so, in 1910 the gold coins were worth twenty dollars."

"You learned all that from your phone? How is that possible?"

"It's easy, I can show you how it works. You can search for anything on the internet and it only takes a few seconds to find it. You don't know about the internet?"

Miss Bristol made a valiant attempt to appear as if she was quite familiar with the internet. "There is no denying that the internet is a marvel, quite astonishing. You can send money to France if you want, and it will be there in a few seconds." She remembered Ben telling her that when he had explained what plastic was.

Silas nodded. "That's true, you can do that."

This new information regarding the price of gold was interesting, but it did nothing to resolve the dilemma of who she was or where she came from. It was possible that when she had lost her memories, she had forgotten the current value of gold. It would make perfect sense that when she saw the original value imprinted on the coin, she naturally assumed that was the coin's current value. There was nothing mysterious about it.

When dinner was done, Miss Bristol insisted that she be the one to do the dishes, that Silas could finish his homework, and Mrs. Wiggins could sit on the couch and relax. "You cooked a lovely dinner, and now it's my turn to help by washing the dishes."

"That's very thoughtful of you, Miss Bristol, but we have a dishwasher. Silas, would you please show Miss Bristol how to use the dishwasher? It can be tricky if you haven't used this model before."

Miss Bristol had no idea what a dishwasher was, once again doing her best to conceal both her lack of knowledge and her astonishment that a machine could wash the dishes.

With the table cleared, and the dishwasher running, Miss Bristol headed up to her room, saying she was tired from her long day. She took a seat in the stuffed armchair, leaning back, her eyes on the television, having no idea how to make the moving images appear. It was odd that she had no knowledge of the device, odd that her amnesia would have caused her to forget everyday things like a television or a dishwasher or microwave. She hadn't forgotten other basic things, like how to open doors, how to walk, how to speak, so why would she forget televisions and dishwashers? She had no answers for this question. The simplest solution for her current dilemma would be to ask Silas how to operate the television, telling him she hadn't operated this model before.

She got up, heading down the stairs, stopping when she heard Silas's raised voice.

"She's not Anna, so don't pretend she is. You can't just replace her with someone else, dress her in Anna's clothes."

"I know that, Silas, I know she's not Anna, and I'm not trying to replace her. That is never going to happen, we both know that. But I can tell you that if Anna had ever run away from home and was living on the streets, I would hope that a family like ours would take her in and treat her with kindness, sharing their home with her. I am only doing what I would wish for Anna, if she was in the same situation as Miss Bristol."

"What is her situation? What's with the weird clothes? I went online and checked out the play about the Gilded Age. There's no one in the play named Miss Bristol; no characters and no actors."

"Clearly she is not an actress. I also know she has

said nothing about her family, or where she's from, or why she's here in New York."

"She doesn't know anything about tech—about smartphones or computers, or video games, or how to use a dishwasher. Who doesn't know that?"

"There are religious communities out there where these things are forbidden. That could explain it. She may have run away from a place like that."

"Like a cult or something? She's not going to murder us is she?"

"You've been watching way too much TV. Maybe she just wanted to see what the rest of the world was like."

"That would explain her old-fashioned clothes, and it goes right along with no tech. You should talk to her, ask her. Maybe some psycho cult leader is chasing after her."

"Again, too much TV. When the time is right, she'll tell us. She's fragile now, trying to fit into a new world. Let's give her some time to adjust, show her some kindness and understanding."

Miss Bristol was stunned; she hadn't fooled them at all. They had known all along that she wasn't an actress, that she knew nothing about devices like televisions and dishwashers.

She crept silently back up the stairs to her room,

lying down on her bed, deciding what to do. After some thought, she decided she would tell them everything, that she had amnesia, that she had no idea who she was or where she came from. They were kind people, and they would understand. But first, she needed to go back to Mama Rosa's Pizza and talk to Ben.

Miss Bristol arrived at Mama Rosa's the following day just before noon, but Ben was nowhere to be seen. She entered the shop, taking a seat on a bench near the door. This time when she gave her order to the clerk, she would be prepared. She watched carefully as people ordered their lunch, listening to what they said, how they said it, how they paid for the pizza, and how they got their change back. This time she had cash in her pocket from the sale of the gold coins. She studied the display sign behind the counter, noting the price of a single slice of pizza. One slice of pepperoni pizza was four dollars. She pulled some bills from her pocket, finding a five dollar bill, then got into the line.

When it was her turn, she stepped up to the counter, slapping the five dollar bill down on the counter. "One slice of pepperoni."

The man nodded, taking the five dollar bill and handing one dollar back in change. He stopped, studying her. "You're the one who tried to pay with that fake gold coin. I recognize your hair."

Miss Bristol had prepared her answer in advance. "I was auditioning for a part in that Gilded Age play. I didn't get the part."

"Don't worry about it, you're not the first actor who didn't get a part. Keep trying, one day you'll be famous." He handed her the slice of pepperoni, calling out, "Next!"

Miss Bristol smiled to herself. That had gone far better than she had expected, and the man had said something encouraging to her, making no comment about her wearing men's trousers. She stepped outside, taking a seat at a table, looking around for Ben. It was noon, but he wasn't there. She decided to wait for him.

A few minutes later an elderly woman wearing a long green woolen coat and gold-rimmed glasses stopped at her table. "Your hair is quite stunning, young lady. You're not a famous actress or a rock star are you?"

Miss Bristol laughed. "I am most certainly not a famous actress." She had no idea what a rock star was.

"Would you mind if I sat with you?"

"Not at all. I am waiting for someone, but they appear to be late."

"A handsome young man, I should imagine?"

"No, much more like a kindly old grandpa. He might not be having lunch here today."

"I adore your hair, you must be Irish."

"I'm afraid I don't know very much about my heritage."

"Not many people do these days, dear. It's a far different world than the one I grew up in. Sometimes I feel like a time traveler who landed smack in the middle of the future. All this modern technology can be quite confusing. I don't know how you young people keep up with all the changes."

"It is just as confusing to me, all the new technology."

"That's good to hear, I don't feel quite so old now. What do you do? Where do you work?"

"I don't have a job at this time, but I am looking for work."

The woman studied Miss Bristol, then said, "I don't know if this would appeal to you at all, but I'm looking for someone to help me take care of my house; cleaning, running a few errands, grocery shopping at the corner store, things of that nature. My husband passed several years ago, and at my age, tasks that used to be simple have become quite difficult for me. I would pay you whatever the current rate is. I live about three blocks from here."

Miss Bristol gave a bright smile. “I should like that, it sounds perfect. I’m renting a room with a lovely family in this area. It would only be a ten or fifteen minute walk for me. I don’t have a car. There’s really no need for one in the city, with the buses and subways and rideshares.” She grinned to herself. She had not mentioned trolleys.

“You are quite correct, young lady. When would you like to start?”

“Whenever you wish.”

“Would you care to walk there with me now? You could see the house, decide if you still want to take the job.”

“I would love to.”

The old woman stood up. “Splendid. I walk slowly, so please be patient with me. I have to use this dreadful cane so I don’t fall on my head, knock myself silly.” She laughed. “Oh, I am Mrs. Smith.” She reached out, shaking Miss Bristol’s hand.

“It’s a pleasure to meet you, Mrs. Smith. I am Miss Bristol.”

Chapter 4

As they were strolling down the sidewalk, Mrs. Smith said, “The city is so different now, nothing like it was when I was a young girl. I am still living in the house where I grew up, but the neighborhood around us has changed, all our old neighbors are long gone. These days I keep to myself most of the time. It seems as soon as I get to know the neighbors, they move on and a new family takes their place. So many have come and gone over the years. Did you grow up in the city?”

“No, I arrived recently and rented a room near here. The city is far larger than I had imagined. It can be quite confusing.”

“Quite true. I think you’ll discover that neighborhoods are like small villages. We used to know everyone in ours, shopping together at the corner store, saying hello to each other when we put the trash cans out, or walked the dog. It seems like an enormous city, but the neighborhoods can be quite cozy.”

"That sounds quite pleasant."

"What made you decide to move to the big city, Miss Bristol?"

"I don't really know, I just found myself here and decided to stay."

"I understand, life is never a straight line, as they say. I can tell you that things always work out in the end, no matter how difficult they seem to be at the time. There have been times when it felt as though I was being guided by fate. At least that's how I felt when I met my dear husband Albert. It was fate that brought us together, of that I have no doubt."

Mrs. Smith's house was much larger than Miss Bristol had anticipated, a single three-story home with its own driveway, private garage, and a lovely yard and garden surrounded by a tall wrought iron fence.

"Your home is beautiful."

"Thank you, dear. It's quite old, built in 1869, but it has been modernized somewhat over the years, mostly the electrical and plumbing systems. The inside looks much as it did a hundred years ago. I will admit there is something comforting about having a home that ignores time, even as the world outside is changing every day."

That was the moment Miss Bristol decided she liked Mrs. Smith.

The instant she stepped inside, Miss Bristol felt at home. “This is lovely, so cozy.”

“Thank you. It’s quite a sight right now, I’m afraid, so much to do, so many things to be tidied up and organized. I’ve been quite derelict in my duties, I’m afraid.”

Miss Bristol raised her eyebrows when they entered the kitchen, eyeing the stacks of dirty plates and bowls and cups in the sink and on the counter.

Mrs. Smith said, “I apologize for the state of the kitchen. I can’t reach the upper cupboards because of my arthritis, and I don’t have a dishwasher. I never did like the idea of a machine washing my dishes.”

Miss Bristol smiled. “I understand completely. It won’t take long to wash all the dishes and put everything back where it belongs in the cupboards and drawers.”

“Thank you so much, you are a godsend. Cleaning has been such a burden this last year, trying to keep the house in order. It’s been quite discouraging at times.”

Miss Bristol said, “Shall I come by tomorrow morning around ten o’clock? Would that be a suitable time? I should head home now, before Mrs. Wiggins worries about me.”

“That would be perfect. You have no idea what a

great relief this is to me. I feel as if an immense weight has been lifted from my shoulders."

Miss Bristol made the fifteen minute walk home, stepping through the front door, greeted unexpectedly by the sight of a strange man wearing a dark gray suit and tie, standing in the hallway. He turned, looked at her curiously, then smiled. "You must be Miss Bristol, our new tenant. I am Harlan Wiggins. It's a pleasure to meet you. Dorothy has said nothing but nice things about you."

"It is a pleasure to meet you, Mr. Wiggins. Mrs. Wiggins said you are a police detective?"

"Please call me Harlan. And yes, I am a detective with NYPD, for better or worse. How are you coping with life in New York City?"

Miss Bristol was quite certain that Mrs. Wiggins had told her husband everything they suspected about her, that she had run away from home to live in New York. She framed her answer carefully.

"It can be quite confusing, the city is far bigger than I had thought it would be."

"You're from a small town, then?"

"Yes, I suppose you could say that, a small town."

"I imagine you're experiencing some culture shock, but not to worry, it won't be long before you feel right at home in the city."

"Thank you so much for your kindness. I was very lucky to find this room to rent. An old man at Mama Rosa's Pizza said he saw the sign in the window and sent me here. He showed me how to eat pizza like a New Yorker, folding it in half. He's the one who told me to rent a room instead of staying in a hotel."

Harlan laughed. "Yes, folding the pizza, that's a must for any New Yorker. As for the hotel, I don't think anyone but a CEO can afford a hotel room in New York."

Miss Bristol nodded, smiling, having no idea what a CEO was.

Mrs. Wiggins stepped out of the kitchen, saying, "I see you two have met. I hope Harlan is not using his detective voice and interrogating you." She laughed.

Harlan said, "Not at all, we were talking about how to eat pizza and the impossibly high prices of hotel rooms in New York."

Miss Bristol said, "I have some exciting news; I have found employment. I am helping a woman clean and organize her home, running errands, and helping with grocery shopping. She's quite old, and the house is rather large, a three-story home with its own driveway and garage and a lovely fenced yard. I met her at Mama Rosa's Pizza."

"That's wonderful news, good for you."

Harlan said, “She seems trustworthy?”

Mrs. Wiggins laughed. “Ever the detective.”

“Yes, she’s quite trustworthy, a lovely person. She has told me a great deal about her and her home. I sincerely like her.”

Harlan nodded. “Excellent, it sounds like you have everything well in hand then.”

Mrs. Wiggins clapped her hands. “Enough chit-chat, everyone wash their hands, it’s time for dinner.”

They were halfway through dinner when Miss Bristol made her decision. She set her fork down, saying, “I have a confession to make.”

There was a sudden silence, three sets of eyes on her.

Mrs. Wiggins said, “What kind of confession?”

Silas was grinning.

“It’s about who I am, where I come from, and why I’m here.”

Mrs. Wiggins raised her eyebrows. “Who are you?”

“The truth of it is that I don’t know who I am. I have amnesia. The last memory I have is finding myself in an alleyway near the corner of Bogart and Moore Streets. I had a terrible headache and thought I was going to faint or throw up. That’s all I know. I remember nothing else of my past, except my name,

Miss Bristol. I had no identification with me and I was wearing old-fashioned clothes."

Mrs. Wiggins said, "You poor girl, you should have told us this before. You must have been terrified, all alone in the city like that, not knowing where you were?"

"It was quite frightening. I had no idea what to do, or where to go."

Harlan said, "I've worked with amnesia victims before, so I understand how frightening and confusing it can be. First of all, let me assure you that there's nothing for you to worry about. You're in good hands here, you're safe. Not to get too technical, but you could have something called dissociative amnesia, brought on by a traumatic event that your mind wants to forget. Were you injured at all? Any bruises, cuts, anything like that?"

"After about twenty minutes my headache was gone and I felt fine, completely normal."

"No big bumps on your head, no head injuries?"

"Nothing."

"And you have absolutely no memories of who you were?"

"None at all."

"Were you carrying anything with you?"

"An embroidered travel bag, and a newspaper."

"Where was the newspaper from?"

Miss Bristol hesitated. "It would be best if I showed you the newspaper and the travel bag. I'll run upstairs and get them."

Five minutes later Harlan was studying the newspaper, a deeply puzzled look on his face. "It's from 1910. Why do you have a newspaper from 1910?"

"I have no idea." She removed the bottles of hair tonic and face creams from the travel bag, setting them on the table.

Harlan examined them. "They're from the same time period, early nineteen hundreds."

Silas said, "Whoa, maybe you're a time traveler. How cool would that be? Wait, you're not from the future, are you? Did you come back to the wrong time, to 2025 instead of 1910? Are you trying to change the future? Prevent a war, or a virus that turns everyone into zombies?"

Harlan shook his head. "I hate to burst your bubble, but she is not a time traveler. The newspaper is new, a reprint, no more than a few months old, as are the beauty products. Why would you be carrying these?"

"I am at a loss for answers."

"I suppose they could be props from a play, or a movie set, or maybe from one of those historical parks or museums where actors dress in period clothing."

"I don't know why I was carrying them."

"It is curious, but like all mysteries, there is undoubtedly a simple, logical explanation. Would you like me to try to find out who you are? I can run you through the missing persons database, run facial recognition, fingerprints, DNA tests."

"I don't know what any of that means. What is running a facial recognition?"

"It's all relatively new technology. In the past we would have to look though big books of photographs, trying to match your face. Now it's all done on computers, using a vast collection of millions of digital photographs of faces, the computer searching through that database for an image that matches your face in a matter of minutes. DNA is the molecule in your body that carries your specific genetic instructions for the growth of your body. Every living creature has DNA, and each one is unique, like a fingerprint. If we get a sample of your DNA, we can compare it to millions of other samples and more than likely find yours, or the DNA of a close relative."

Mrs. Wiggins gave a comforting smile. "It sounds very complicated, but it's not, and it works. They use it every day to find missing people or to solve crimes. There's nothing to worry about."

Silas said, "I've had a DNA test. It takes two seconds, it's nothing."

Miss Bristol said, "Suppose I discover something dreadful? Suppose I come from a family of murderers, or suppose I have escaped from prison, or robbed a bank?"

Silas grinned. "How cool would that be? Maybe you hid a whole bunch of money and you're running from the mob."

Harlan stared at Silas, then laughed. "You really should be an author."

Mrs. Wiggins reached across the table, taking Miss Bristol's hand. "You may have lost your memory, but you are still you, and I can see that you are a good person who would never hurt anyone."

Miss Bristol was deeply moved by Mrs. Wiggins' kind comment.

Harlan said, "It's up to you. You don't have to do any of this if you don't want to, and if we do find a relative, you don't have to meet them or talk to them. We won't contact them unless you want us to. Sometimes memories come back on their own. You're walking down the street, see something that clicks, and boom, you remember everything. That's happened more than once. When you're ready, your memories will come back to you."

Mrs. Wiggins said, "Thank you for telling us this, Miss Bristol. I know it must have been so difficult for you. Take your time to make a decision about the tests. While you're waiting, you can always make new memories, maybe even better ones."

Silas grinned. "I've never met anyone with amnesia before. Unless I *have* met someone, but I have amnesia. How ironic would that be?"

Mrs. Wiggins gave him a dark look. "Not funny, Silas." She turned to Miss Bristol, saying, "Before I forget, we have a present for you. Silas, would you like to give it to her?"

Silas set a smartphone down on the table, sliding it over to Miss Bristol. "It's my old phone, I got a new one. I can show you how to use it, how to make calls and send text messages."

Mrs. Wiggins nodded. "Carry it with you always, and call us whenever you want. If you need anything at all, call us. Let us know if you're going to be late coming home from your new job so we don't worry."

Miss Bristol picked up the phone, staring at it. "You're giving this to me? A phone?"

"We are. It's yours to keep. Everyone has one now; we all carry them around with us whether we like it or not."

Silas added, "And you can research anything on

the internet. It's easy, I can show you that too."

"I don't know how to thank you."

Mrs. Wiggins said, "You don't have to. You're safe here, always remember that."

Miss Bristol nodded, afraid she might cry.

The following morning Miss Bristol set off for Mrs. Smith's house, her new smartphone tucked into her jeans pocket. Silas had showed her how to make phone calls and send texts and emails, giving her all their phone numbers and email addresses. He had her send him a text and call him from her room while he was downstairs in the kitchen. He also showed her how to search for information on the internet, and how to carry the phone in her pocket so she'd look cool, explaining to her what cool meant.

She smiled as she strolled along, her hand pressing against the smartphone in her jeans pocket. It was hard to believe; she was wearing jeans, she had her own phone, she knew what pizza was, how to eat it correctly, she was looking cool, and she was living in New York City in 2025.

Miss Bristol arrived at Mrs. Smith's house promptly at ten o'clock, spotting Mrs. Smith peering out the window, waving to her. Miss Bristol unlatched the heavy iron gate, swinging it open, closing it behind her. She headed up the walkway, the front door opening, Mrs. Smith greeting her.

"Good morning, Miss Bristol, you're quite punctual, arriving precisely when you said you would."

Miss Bristol said, "It's only a fifteen minute walk from the house where I am staying." She stepped inside, saying, "First things first, we shall get the kitchen in order, then move on to the rest of the house."

Mrs. Smith put her hand on Miss Bristol's arm. "I can't thank you enough for helping me. I'm normally very wary about having people in the house whom I have just met, but it is the oddest thing; the moment I saw you, I knew I could trust you. Isn't that strange?"

Miss Bristol nodded. "I have learned to trust feelings such as those." She stopped, thinking about what she had just said. Where had she learned that? Why had she said that?

Chapter 5

They headed into the kitchen, Miss Bristol spending the next three hours washing dishes, drying them, stacking them neatly in the cupboards, mopping the floor, scrubbing the counters, cleaning the refrigerator, throwing out any old food, and making a list of any groceries that were needed. When she was done, she called in Mrs. Smith, who was thrilled beyond measure when she saw the immaculately clean kitchen.

"Good heavens, you are a miracle worker, Miss Bristol. I have never seen the kitchen so clean and tidy before."

"What would you like me to start on now?"

"How about I give you a tour of the house, and you can decide for yourself?"

"That sounds wonderful."

They walked through the house, Miss Bristol feeling as though she was traveling back in time to Mrs. Smith's childhood, hearing a hundred stories about her family, the history of the home and all the adventures they had growing up here. Her grandparents had built the house, and it had been passed down through three generations.

"It was a different time, things were slower, people didn't move around all the time back then. It was quite common for two or three generations of family members to be living in the same home, all taking care of each other. I have such fond memories of this house." She stopped, a wistful look in her eyes. "Except for the day my father disappeared."

"Your father disappeared?"

"He did, and we never saw him again."

"That's quite dreadful. You never learned what happened to him?"

"Follow me, Miss Bristol, I have something to show you."

They headed up the staircase to the second floor, walking down a narrow hallway to a closed door, Mrs. Smith pushing it open.

Miss Bristol studied the long glass display case filled with antiquities and ancient artifacts. "What are all these things?"

"My father was a professor at Columbia University. He also loved to read about archeology, mostly Mesoamerican civilizations; Olmec, Aztec, Mayan, and a number of others. Some of these relics he brought back with him from a dig he went on in 1910 with several friends from the anthropology department."

Miss Bristol was getting a curious feeling, an urge to open the glass case and examine the relics, to touch them. She turned to a grouping of framed photographs on the wall, old sepia tone images of ancient stone ruins. "These photographs are wonderful."

"My father took those pictures with an old folding Kodak camera on his 1910 expedition. Back then you had to mail the camera in to Kodak to get your film developed and get prints."

Miss Bristol studied one of the images, pointing to it. "That is The Temple of the Feathered Serpent."

"Good heavens, dear, you're quite right. How did you ever know that? It's in Teotihuacan. That was where my father went on the dig with his friends."

"I have no idea how I knew such a thing. The words just popped into my head when I saw it."

"You must have seen a picture of it sometime in the past, and it came back to you. I have had that happen, had something pop into my head that I hadn't thought about in years. Father used to say that we permanently store all our memories, but as we get older it becomes harder to retrieve them. Perhaps it was something you studied in school."

"That must be what it was."

"My father was ninety-one years old when he disappeared, back in 1972. I came home from work and he was gone. There was no note, and they never found him. The police said he must have wandered off, but I know he would not have done that. He was a little eccentric at times, but he was as smart as a whip, alert and aware. He would not have wandered off and gotten lost."

"I'm so sorry, that must have been dreadful. Were you close to him?"

"I was. He was a wonderful father, always encouraging us, telling us the world was a miracle. He also said that to know our past is to know our future. Perhaps that's why he enjoyed reading about ancient civilizations."

"He sounds like a lovely man."

"He was. I don't know why he didn't leave us a note. It doesn't make sense. It wasn't like him to do something like that."

"The police found no trace of him?"

"There was no evidence of foul play, the front door was locked, his office clean and tidy. Nothing was missing except him."

Miss Bristol was silent, her eyes roaming across

the room, coming to rest on a glass cabinet holding several heavy leather-bound volumes. "Are those journals of his?"

"They are old photographs. I keep them locked up. I can't bear to look at them. I always think that if I had come home from work earlier that day, I might have prevented whatever happened."

"It sounds as if he left of his own accord, waiting until you were at work."

"You might be right. I suppose you can never know the deepest feelings of anyone, even your own father. I just wish I could have helped him."

They headed back downstairs, Miss Bristol spending the rest of the day cleaning the living room and dining room, Mrs. Smith showing her how to use the old Hoover canister vacuum cleaner.

At four o'clock she used her new phone to call Mrs. Wiggins, telling her she was on her way home. Mrs. Smith's father was right, the world was a miracle, and so was her new smartphone.

Four days later, while they were having dinner, Miss Bristol said to Harlan, "I should like you to run your tests. I have decided I would like to know who I am."

Harlan said, "What made you decide to do this?"

"I remembered something, but I have no idea how

I knew it."

"Something about your past?"

"When I was at Mrs. Smith's, she was showing me her father's study. He was a professor at Columbia University. There was a photograph of an ancient stone temple on the wall that he had taken in 1910. When I saw it, I knew instantly that it was The Temple of the Feathered Serpent, and Mrs. Smith said I was correct. I have no idea how I knew that, but I want to find out. It might have something to do with who I am."

Silas grabbed his phone, tapping on it. "It's in Teotihuacan, Mexico. There's some pyramids there: Pyramid of the Moon, Pyramid of the Sun, and The Temple of the Feathered Serpent. Super old, over two thousand years. The Aztecs found it after it had been abandoned for about three hundred years."

Harlan said, "Does that ring any bells?"

"I don't know. I don't think so."

"I have a box of DNA swab tests in my travel kit. There's nothing to it—I just swab the inside of your cheek for the test. I'll take it to work, send it to a lab where they extract the DNA and analyze your genetic markers. Once that's done, we compare your markers to those in a huge genetic database. That should identify any close relatives, but only if their DNA is in the database. We usually find something, even if it's a distant relative. We'll also be able to identify your ancestry, although your orange hair kind of gives that away. I'll go out on a limb and say you have Irish ancestors."

Mrs. Wiggins said, "You have lovely orange eyes. You're not wearing orange contacts are you?"

Miss Bristol shook her head. "I am not. I think my eyes are just orange. I don't even know what contacts are."

Harlan said, "Interesting, we'll see what the DNA guys say about that. It could be a unique marker."

He took three photos of Miss Bristol with his phone, saying, "We'll run these through our facial recognition database, see what we find. If we don't get any hits on that, we'll do a reverse image search across the internet. If you have any internet presence at all, we'll find out who you are—and just for the record, everyone has an internet presence. In the unlikely event that we don't find anything, we'll try a different tack, maybe go to a neurologist, get a CT scan of your brain, check for any damage, anything not right."

"I don't want anyone poking about in my brain."

"They don't touch your brain, they scan it, look for anything that might be causing the amnesia. It's unlikely, but you may have had a stroke."

Miss Bristol shook her head. “I don’t want any of that, it sounds frightening.”

“Not a problem, it’s just an option. We’ll cross that bridge when we get to it.”

Miss Bristol spent the following morning at Mrs. Smith’s house, cleaning the downstairs sitting room and the parlor. She also spent a great deal of time worrying what Harlan Wiggins would discover about her past, imagining all manner of frightful possibilities. Suppose she was a murderess, or a thief, or a spy, or a madwoman escaped from an asylum? What would happen to her then? Where would she go? Her most fervent hope was that she had a loving family who missed her and was desperately searching for her, a family like the Wiggins.

The unexpected results of Harlan’s search for her identity arrived five days later at the dinner table.

Harlan took a seat at the table, setting down a sheath of papers. “I have news, Miss Bristol, but it was not the news I had hoped for. I have the results of your DNA comparison test, facial recognition search, and fingerprint comparisons. Unfortunately, none of them gave any definitive results. We still have no idea who you are. Your DNA tests confirmed that you do have Irish heritage, as we suspected, but it was unable to locate any close relatives, only very, very distant possibilities, and even those are uncertain at best. I can tell you that this is most unusual, and I have no explanation for it. Facial recognition found no matching faces in the database, and you have no internet presence. There were no hits on fingerprints either. In short, you are a mystery, Miss Bristol, an enigma. We are no closer to discovering your identity than we were five days ago. There are other search mechanisms we can try, using your name for instance, but I can't guarantee anything. We may be forced to wait until your memory returns. You don't speak any other languages, do you?"

Miss Bristol shook her head. "I don't think so."

Silas said, "Parlez-vous Francais? Habla Español?"

"I'm quite certain I don't know any other languages." She turned to Harlan. "Thank you for your efforts. I am disappointed, but also somewhat relieved by this news. I'm uncertain if I truly do want to know my past, especially if the cause of my memory loss was a dreadful traumatic event."

"I understand. Perhaps we should wait, not press the matter any further. When the time is right, your memories will return."

That evening Miss Bristol spent almost an hour playing Zombie Apocalypse with Silas, blasting the undead, laughing.

The words came out of nowhere, surprising Miss Bristol. "Your mother told me about Anna."

Silas glanced over at her, saying nothing.

Miss Bristol set down the controller. "What was she like?"

Silas shrugged. "She told me to study more, said I was a math genius."

"She must have been proud of you."

"I guess. It should have been me, not her. She was better at stuff than me. She had way more friends, everyone liked her. It should have been me. I only have a few friends."

Miss Bristol was filled with an immense sadness. "We don't get to choose such things, Silas. They simply happen, and then we are left alone, trying to understand why." Miss Bristol was afraid she might cry.

Silas looked at her. "Are you all right?"

"I don't know, I may have lost someone, someone very dear to me. Why can't I remember?"

"You don't know who it was?"

Miss Bristol shook her head. "How could I forget someone I loved? How could I do such a thing? What kind of person am I?"

"Maybe that's what gave you amnesia, maybe that

was the traumatic event. You're lucky, I wish I could forget."

"It is far worse not remembering. Anna still lives in your thoughts, your memories. She still talks to you, you still hear her voice, telling you to study, telling you you're a math genius. Whoever I lost is gone to me, as though they never were. How could I forget someone I loved, betray them like that?"

"It's not your fault, it's the amnesia."

"That is kind of you to say."

"Anna used to say I'd make a good mad scientist, that I should major in physics at college."

Miss Bristol managed a smile. "Perhaps you shall be the one to invent time travel."

"I wish I could. I wish I could go back in time."

Mrs. Wiggins called out from the kitchen, "Silas, do you have homework?"

"I'm working on it now, I only have a thousand more zombies to kill."

"Not funny."

Miss Bristol whispered, "You make your mom laugh."

The next morning Miss Bristol left early for Mrs. Smith's home. There was a lot to do and she wanted to get started. Mrs. Smith was gone for the day, off to a special showing at the American Museum of Natural

History, a number of the artifacts being displayed having been donated to the museum by her father.

Miss Bristol was vacuuming under the ornate sofa in the sitting room when there was a sudden clunking sound, the vacuum hose clogged by an unknown object. She shut off the vacuum and pulled the hose out, examining it. There was a rock jammed into the end of the hose. When she pulled it out she saw it was more than just a rock, it was a carved stone figure, and it was old.

She studied it closely, turning it over in her hand. Interesting, it was Tláloc the Rain God, from the Temple of the Feathered Serpent.

She froze, her eyes riveted on the figure, her thoughts spinning. This was impossible, it could not be so. How could she know this?

She gripped the stone figure tightly in her hand, stepping into the foyer and darting up the stairs to the artifact room, pushing the door open, clicking the light on. She scanned the glass case, her eyes coming to rest on a stone carving. It was larger than the one in her hand, but it was clearly the same figure. She read the small handwritten placard next to the figure.

Tláloc the Rain God

The god of rain in Aztec religion, also a deity of

earthly fertility and water, worshipped as a giver of life and sustenance. Tláloc was mainly worshiped at Teotihuacan, although important rituals were held on Cerro Tláloc. An underground Tláloc shrine has been discovered at Teotihuacan.

Miss Bristol carefully raised the lid of the glass case, setting the small stone carving of Tláloc next to the larger one, then closed the lid, studying the figures. She realized then that it was no accident she was in this house, that she was looking at these artifacts. She remembered what Mrs. Smith had said—there were times when she felt as if she was being guided by fate, by unseen forces.

Miss Bristol took a seat in an old leather office chair, studying the case of artifacts. The question was, why had these unseen forces guided her to this house? Clearly she had some past knowledge of Mesoamerican antiquities, but from where? Where could she possibly have learned about such things? She was only nineteen or twenty years old. There had to be someone out there who knew her, a family member, or friends, or people she had worked with. She had to have known someone before she lost her memory.

She pulled her phone from her pocket, checking the time. It was almost noon. She would go to Mama

Rosa's Pizza and talk to Ben. He had told her, "First things first, rent a room, a cozy safe place." Without his advice, none of these events would have occurred. Maybe he could help her navigate this baffling new situation—her inexplicable knowledge of Mesoamerican relics.

Chapter 6

She headed down the stairs and out the front door, locking it behind her, walking briskly toward Mama Rosa's Pizza.

Ben was not there when she arrived, so she stepped into the shop, pulling a five dollar bill from her pocket, standing in line. She was both surprised and not surprised when she heard the familiar voice coming from behind her, turning around to see Ben.

"Miss Bristol, a pleasure to see you today. I trust you are doing well?"

"I am doing quite well, thank you for asking. As a matter of fact, I was hoping to see you here. I need your advice on a rather concerning matter."

"I will do the best I can, but advice is only advice, nothing more than one person's opinion."

"I understand completely, but renting a room has sent me down a rather curious path, and a most baffling one."

"That sounds quite intriguing. Shall we sit

outside?"

With pizzas in hand, Miss Bristol and Ben headed out the door, finding an empty table, Miss Bristol enjoying the warmth of the noonday sun.

"A lovely day today, is it not?" Ben smiled at her.

"It is a lovely day. There is something I must confess to you."

"I'm all ears, as they say."

"I am not an actress and I have never been one. I have amnesia, no idea of who I am, or how I came to be in New York."

"This is quite distressing news, Miss Bristol."

The curious thing was, Ben did not seem to be the least bit surprised by her revelation. She wondered if perhaps after a certain age there were no surprises left to be had. The more likely answer was that he had seen through her charade as quickly as Mrs. Wiggins had.

Miss Bristol continued, "I have no memory of how I came to be here, or why I was wearing those old-fashioned clothes from the Gilded Age."

"I see. You have absolutely no memories at all, not even one?"

"That is why I wished to see you. There is a memory, but I have no understanding of it."

"We shall start with that, then."

"I am working for a woman named Mrs. Smith. She is quite old and needed help taking care of her home, a lovely three-story house built in 1869. Her father was a professor at Columbia University who liked to collect ancient Mesoamerican artifacts. There is a long glass display case in his office holding dozens of artifacts he collected over the years. There was a photograph hanging on the wall, a stone temple he had visited in 1910. When I saw the photograph, without hesitation, I identified it correctly as the Temple of the Feathered Serpent."

Ben raised his eyebrows. "This is very curious."

"There's more to the story. This morning as I was vacuuming beneath a sofa in Mrs. Smith's house, I found a small stone figurine. Again, without a thought, I identified it correctly as Tláloc the Rain God, from the Temple of the Feathered Serpent."

Ben was silent, his eyes resting on Miss Bristol.

"How is it possible that I was able to identify such things?"

"It is quite obvious, I should imagine. These things must have been known to you before you lost you memory. The sight of them stirred something inside you, causing you to remember."

"But I've never been to that house before. I only met Mrs. Smith recently, in the last few weeks."

"Perhaps you have been there before, but you have forgotten."

"Surely if that were so, Mrs. Smith would have remembered me, recognized my orange hair."

"A valid point. I suppose it's also possible that you studied about Mesoamerican cultures in school, perhaps even at university level."

"I am too young to have studied such things at university level. As you suggested, I rented a room from Mrs. Wiggins. Her husband, Harlan, is a detective with the New York Police Department, and has been attempting to discover my identity, but as yet has found nothing, even after DNA tests and facial recognition searches."

Ben raised his eyebrows. "I'm impressed, Miss Bristol, you seem to be adapting quite well to your current circumstances."

"The Wiggins have shown me great kindness and understanding. They even gave me a phone, their son Silas teaching me how to use it."

"Some people are accepted to university at quite an early age. Do you like Mrs. Smith? Does she seem nice? Do you feel comfortable in her home?"

"I do. I trusted her the moment I saw her. She is a lovely woman."

"Excellent. Would you like a little more of my

grandfatherly advice?"

"I would welcome it with all my heart."

Ben said, "You feel comfortable and safe in Mrs. Smith's home, and that is good. You are relaxed there, letting your thoughts wander as they will, a few of them returning to you with memories of your past, memories brought on by the artifacts from Teotihuacan. I would suggest that you spend more time perusing the antiquities there—perhaps it will trigger the return of more memories, perhaps all of them. Such things are entirely within the realm of possibility."

Miss Bristol studied the old man's face. "You have helped me more than you can imagine. I am deeply indebted to you."

"I consider you a friend, Miss Bristol, and friends help each other as best they can."

"I also consider you to be a friend. I will do as you say and let you know if any more memories return to me."

When Miss Bristol returned to Mrs. Smith's home she ran up the stairs to the artifact room, swinging the door open. She took a seat in the leather chair, taking a deep breath, letting it out slowly, trying to relax, letting her mind wander. She got up, stepping over to the display case, reading the placards, studying the ancient figurines and relics closely. There was a curious familiarity about them.

She opened the case, picking up the artifacts one by one, holding them in her hand, pressing them against her face, feeling the coolness of the stone, the rough textures. When she had held them all, she closed the display case, taking a seat again, closing her eyes, trying to remember, letting her thoughts wander. She imagined a bright sun, trying to see The Temple of the Feathered Serpent in her thoughts, imagining herself standing in front of it, imagining her clothes, the dust, a soft warm breeze. She opened her eyes, looking around the room, her eyes stopping on the locked glass case holding the leather bound photo albums that were so distressing to Mrs. Smith.

She stood up, approaching the glass cabinet, a strange tingling sensation running through her when she pressed her hand against the glass. Was she being guided?

She attempted to turn the latch, but it was locked, just as Mrs. Smith had said. There must be a key somewhere. She spent the next fifteen minutes searching through drawers, through the oak roll-top desk, but found nothing. She glanced at the cabinet again, walking over to it, peering behind it, spotting a small silver key hanging from a nail. She grabbed it, stepping around to the front of the cabinet, inserting the key, twisting it, her efforts rewarded by a soft click of the lock, the glass door swinging open.

She placed a hand on one of the albums, then pulled it out, taking a seat in the leather chair, studying the cover. She took a deep breath and flipped it open, eyeing the old sepia-toned prints. She slowly turned the pages, studying the images. There was an old-fashioned steamship, people dressed in long dark coats and top hats gazing out at a rolling sea, a port city, docks bustling with crowds of people. She saw lush jungles, a curious snake, a steam locomotive billowing clouds of dark smoke.

She was interrupted by the sound of the front door opening, quickly closing the album and putting it back in the cabinet, locking it again and heading downstairs.

"Hello, Miss Bristol, how is your day going?"

"Very well, thank you. How was the showing at the museum?"

"It was lovely, people said such nice things about my father and the artifacts he donated. Something rather peculiar happened, however. The curator said he had been researching my father's 1910 expedition to Teotihuacan so he could write more about him for the display. He contacted the anthropology department at

Columbia, asking about my father and the 1910 expedition. He said a staff member called him back the next day saying they could find only a single brief notation in the records from 1910 mentioning an expedition to Teotihuacan. It said that three crates of artifacts had been brought back. That was all there was; there was no information about who went, no mention of my father, no journals, no maps, nothing. The staff member said it was most unusual, because very detailed records are always kept of all the expeditions, including all the maps and journals and photographs. For some unknown reason, the records of my father's expedition were missing."

Miss Bristol said, "That is odd. Are you certain that's when your father went?"

"Quite certain. I thought perhaps I should look through the two photo albums in Father's office again, look for information about the expedition. I think some of the photos had notations beneath them—possibly names and dates, or where the photo was taken. It's been a long time since I looked at them."

Miss Bristol nodded. "That's an excellent idea. I would be happy to look through them for you, if you would like me to."

"That would be wonderful, if you could do that. I don't enjoy looking through those old photos, seeing

Father when he was a young man. It makes me dreadfully sad. Why don't you take the rest of the afternoon and look through them, writing down any names or dates you find, anything at all that might be of interest to the curator at the museum."

"I would love to. I'll start right now."

Miss Bristol headed back upstairs to Professor Wexley's office, opening the cabinet and removing both albums, setting them on the table, grabbing a pad of paper and a pencil. She took a seat, opening the first one, slowly turning the pages. She noted the name of the steamship shown in one photo; the *SS Merida*. There was a notation beneath the photograph.

New York Harbor, June 4, 1910. On our way!

This was good information; she knew the date of their departure, and the name of the steamship they had sailed on. She turned the pages slowly, soon realizing that the first album held only photos of Professor Wexley's journey to Teotihuacan—pictures of the ship, the port of Veracruz, numerous images of Spanish baroque buildings, dense jungles, and a steam locomotive. There was a photo of Professor Wexley posing with an old bearded man, holding up a book, possibly in a restaurant, maybe on the steamship, but she couldn't make out the book's title.

Miss Bristol turned the page, studying the image of a well-dressed young man in what appeared to be a busy train station. He was holding a large basket of fruit, a broad smile on his face.

Arthur's basket of fruit —enough for an army!

Miss Bristol studied the man's face curiously. There was something about it, the way he was smiling—it was the face of someone you could trust.

The next photo was of a formation of soldiers marching down a wide boulevard lined with enormous buildings.

Mexico City, June 13, 1910
Rumors of revolution abound

On the last page was a photo of several people climbing up into a large oddly shaped horse-drawn carriage.

June 14, 1910
Hoorah! Boarding the omnibus to Teotihuacan!

Miss Bristol closed the album, setting it to one

side. She knew now that Professor Wexley had traveled to Teotihuacan with someone named Arthur in June of 1910. That was something—perhaps the department of anthropology at Columbia University could search their records for a man named Arthur who worked there in 1910.

Miss Bristol opened the second album to a large photograph of rough-looking men wearing wide-brimmed canvas hats, digging in the parched earth near a large stepped pyramid, the top of it being flat and level.

June 20, 1910

Pyramid of the Sun - the tunnel excavation begins

She slowly turned the pages, studying the photos from Teotihuacan: the entrance to a dark tunnel; a disheveled man smoking a cigar; three white canvas tents; a group of rough-looking laborers carrying pickaxes and shovels; and a smiling man holding up a heavy revolver. She recognized him as Arthur, the man who had been holding the basket of fruit in the train station photograph.

Without knowing why, Miss Bristol touched his face as she read the note beneath the image.

Arthur and his Webley .455
"Some of the snakes have two legs."

She closed her eyes for a moment, feeling faint, a strange warmth running through her. Those words were so familiar, she had heard someone say them before—she could almost hear his voice. Some of the snakes have two legs. She was close, she could feel it. Something was happening to her.

She turned the page, studying a large photograph of a woman dressed in wrinkled khaki clothes and lace-up leather boots standing between two young men in front of The Temple of the Feathered Serpent. They were smiling, the woman holding up a small stone figurine. Miss Bristol read the pencil notation beneath the photograph, her hands going limp.

Miss Bristol, Arthur, and I
at the Temple of the Feathered Serpent
July 19, 1910

She was the woman in the photograph—she had been there in 1910, smiling, standing next to The Temple of the Feathered Serpent. It was her, there was no doubt.

Another wave of heat rolled up through her body,

the air shimmering, the ground trembling, a pale green mist surrounding her. She leaned over, afraid she might faint, gripping the table tightly.

This was the singular moment when Miss Bristol remembered everything; a deluge of ten thousand crystal clear memories flooding through her. She knew who she was, who Arthur was, where she came from, and how she came to be in New York City in the year 2025.

Chapter 7

"It is possible to believe that all the human mind has ever accomplished is but the dream before the awakening."
— H.G. Wells

Arthur

Arthur staggered to his feet, pressing one hand against the side of his face, rivulets of blood running down his arm. The headache was unbearable—he'd thrown up, then passed out, hitting the side of his head on a jagged block of concrete. He leaned against the brick wall, studying the shadowy alleyway, confused, no idea where he was.

He walked unsteadily forward, stepping out of the alleyway to a wide city street lined with tall brick buildings, a stream of odd looking vehicles rolling past. The world was spinning again, the nausea returning. He twisted to one side, pressing both hands against the rough surface of the building, trying to steady himself, trying to stop the spinning.

A black and white NYPD patrol car stopped at the curb, twenty feet away from Arthur, the spinning red light on its roof flashing silently. A bright spotlight from the car blinked on, startling Arthur. Two uniformed police officers climbed out, Arthur turning when he heard the car doors close, the spotlight blinding him, illuminating his bloody face. He covered his eyes, the glaring light making his pounding headache even worse.

One of the officers called out, “Hey, buddy, you okay?”

Arthur blocked the light with one hand, trying to see who was talking to him. “Who are you? What do you want?”

They approached slowly, cautiously, one of the officers resting his hand on a holstered revolver.

“Take it easy, pal, we’re cops. You high? On acid? Bad trip?”

“I do not understand your questions, sir.”

“What happened to your face? You get mugged?”

“I fell, struck my head soundly on a concrete block. I have a vicious headache, rendering me faint and quite nauseous.”

"You're not high, no drugs?"

"I fell, hitting my head. I don't know where I am, how I came to be in this place. I can't remember."

"You don't know where you are?"

Arthur shook his head. "I do not."

"What's your name, buddy?"

He tried to focus, tried to remember, but could not. "I don't know. I don't know my own name. What has happened to me?"

"You don't know where you are, and you don't know who you are? You got a wallet, a driver's license?"

"I don't think I have ever driven an automobile. I am not certain if I have ever even ridden in one."

The taller officer turned to his partner. "10-96 maybe. Radio for a wagon, let's get him to Bellevue, get him stitched up, run a psych eval."

"Roger that." The second officer headed back to the squad car, grabbing the microphone from the dash, pressing the PTT button.

"Eight-Three Adam to Central, send a wagon for probable EDP at Bogart and Moore, transport to Bellevue. Head injury, probable concussion, needs EMT."

He exited the patrol car, stepping back over to Arthur, saying, "The ambulance is on its way, pal.

They'll take you to Bellevue Hospital. Docs will take care of you there, check you out, see what's going on."

"My headache is almost gone, but I am still light headed."

"Do you remember who you are?"

Arthur shook his head. "I do not."

"That's a good sign that your headache is gone, but the docs need to take a look at you. You're certain you didn't take any drugs; no weed, smack, mescaline, speed, no nothing?"

"I don't think I drink alcohol."

"Okay, buddy, we'll wait here with you till the ambulance arrives. What kind of suit is that? What's the white collar for? You a priest or something?"

"I don't think so."

The tall officer laughed. "He ain't a priest, that's an old timey collar. My grandpa showed me pictures of him wearing a suit like that when he was young, starched white collar and black tie. That's what they used to wear back then. He said the collar hurt his neck."

The other officer shrugged. "Either way he needs a doc and a psych eval. There's a problem if he's dressed like your grandpa."

Twenty minutes later Arthur was seated in the back

of an ambulance as it maneuvered through the busy New York City streets, making its way toward Bellevue Hospital.

The uniformed EMT facing him gave him a reassuring smile."Okay, I've cleaned you up and bandaged you. Doc's gonna have to give you a couple stitches for the cut, but you probably won't have a scar. You'll be fine, could have been a lot worse. The officers said you can't remember who you are?"

Arthur shook his head. "I have no idea how I came to be in that alleyway, and for the life of me, I can't remember my own name."

"They'll check you out for a concussion; that can cause temporary memory loss. You don't have any obvious bumps on your head, though. It looks like you just scraped your face real bad."

"I had a headache, it made me faint, throw up."

"Maybe a migraine, they can do that, make you sick. You'll be okay."

"I hope so."

"Let me ask you this, do you know who the president is?"

Arthur shook his head. "I have no idea."

"How about what year it is?"

Arthur pressed his hand to his forehead, trying to think, trying to remember. "1910?"

The EMT wrote something in his notebook. "Okay, pal, we're almost there."

A nurse in a white cap and starched uniform stepped out of the Emergency Room entrance, waiting until the ambulance had come to a halt, the EMT emerging from the back of the vehicle. The nurse peered into the ambulance, her eyes on Arthur. "What do we have?"

"Fell and scraped his face, bad headache, maybe migraine, fainted, nauseous, can't remember who he is, where he's from or what year it is. He thought maybe it was 1910. Pulse and BP are elevated, but that's to be expected."

"Okay, let's get him inside, check him out. Sounds like a possible concussion with memory loss."

"That's what I thought, but I'm not seeing any head trauma."

"We'll check him out, see what's going on."

Two hours later, after three stitches and a thorough examination, the doctor said, "I'm not seeing any obvious signs of a concussion, no serious head injuries. Your headache is gone, blood pressure and pulse are normal, you're calm and coherent, no speech problems, arms and legs all moving fine, motor skills are normal, no symptoms of a stroke, no sign of drugs or alcohol. Do you know if you get migraine headaches?"

"I don't think so."

The doctor set his pad down, turning to the nurse. "Let's get him up to neurology, get an evaluation, see what they say. I'm not seeing any obvious physical reasons for his memory loss."

Another three hours passed, Arthur finding himself seated in a chair facing Bellevue's resident psychiatrist. The psychiatrist was leaning forward, assessing Arthur. "How are you feeling, young man?"

"My headache is gone, as is my dizziness and my nausea. To be quite honest, I feel quite normal."

"But you can't remember who you are?"

"I have no idea who I am or where I came from."

"Can you recall any traumatic events you might have experienced recently? The loss of a loved one, a car accident, witnessing a violent crime? Anything like that?"

Arthur shook his head. "Nothing comes to mind."

"Any idea why you'd be wearing an old-fashioned suit and tie?"

"I was wearing it when I found myself in the alleyway."

"All right. I don't see any obvious physical problems, but your amnesia is concerning. Sometimes when a person experiences a traumatic event, their mind blocks it out so they don't have to remember it, they don't have to face it. Often times they forget the event, which is called psychogenic amnesia, but they can also forget who they are, which is called biographical amnesia. The good news is that with time, there is a very good chance that your memory will return. Sometimes it happens in bits and pieces, a memory here and there, and sometimes it happens all at once. I'd like to keep you here for two days, under observation, just to make certain you're stable. You don't have any family or friends that you can recall?"

Arthur shook his head. "None that I know of."

"Well, since you have no family, if your memory doesn't return while you're here, the best thing for you would be a supervised group home, with people who can provide any assistance you might need."

"Is it possible that friends or relatives might try to locate me?"

"It's very possible. If anyone contacts the police or the hospitals looking for you, we will contact you immediately. You're certain you can't remember your name?"

No one was more surprised than Arthur at his answer. "It's Arthur. My name is Arthur. It just popped into my head out of nowhere. How curious."

"That's excellent; a good sign. We have a

photograph of you, and now we have your first name. Take it slow, just relax. I'll come talk to you tomorrow, Arthur."

Two days passed without the return of his memories, Arthur still at a loss as to who he was and how he came to be in the alleyway.

Other than his memory loss, the doctor declared him to be in sound health, and no threat to either himself or anyone else, releasing him to social services.

The next day Arthur moved into a group home in Brooklyn, joining eight other residents, all with some form of disability or condition requiring daily assistance and supervision.

A social worker took Arthur to the home, stepping inside with him, introducing him to one of the caretakers, a man wearing jeans and a tee shirt.

"Hi, Jeremy. This is Arthur, the young man with biographical amnesia I called you about."

Jeremy smiled, shaking Arthur's hand. "It's nice to meet you, Arthur. How are you feeling today? Any of your memories come back to you?"

Arthur shook his head. "They have not."

"It can take a while, especially if you experienced an extremely traumatic event. Take your time, relax. You're safe here. I'm going to have you share a room with a young man about your age. It will be good for you to have someone to talk to, maybe stir up some of those lost memories."

Jeremy led Arthur down a hallway, knocking on a door, a voice calling out, "Enter."

Jeremy opened the door, Arthur stepping into the room, eyeing the man stretched out on a worn couch reading a book.

"Hey, Sky, this is Arthur, your new roommate."

The man named Sky had exceptionally long tangled hair, a fringed suede jacket, bell-bottom jeans and a strikingly colorful tie-dyed tee shirt. The man stared at Arthur, then said, "Nice suit. What's your bag, man?"

"I beg your pardon?"

"You beg my pardon?"

"I'm afraid I don't understand your question, sir. What is a bag?"

"Far out, my roomie is a space cadet."

"A what?"

"Space cadet, that's a good thing. You're out there, man. I dig your suit."

Jeremy said, "Okay, I'll leave you to it." He stepped out of the room, Arthur uncertain if Sky was insulting him or complimenting him. He was also trying to make sense of the man's clothing.

"Your shirt is quite startling, supremely colorful,

but pleasing in its way, I suppose."

"It's called tie-dye. Where you from, Mars?"

"Sadly, I have no idea where I am from. I have what the doctor called biographical amnesia. I remembered my name was Arthur, but I am unable to remember my last name."

The young man sat up, studying Arthur with new eyes. " Isn't that something, biographical amnesia. Interesting. I'll call you King Arthur. Problem solved."

"Why on earth would you call me that?"

"Your first name is King, your last name Arthur. Now you have two names, just like everyone else."

"I see, quite clever. I do have a curious recollection of reading something about someone named King Arthur, but it's hazy. I appreciate your efforts, sir, and I thank you. How should I address you?"

"Call me Sky."

"Would that be your first name or last name?"

"I'm just Sky, nothing but Sky. I'm nowhere and everywhere."

"I see, quite profound indeed, sir. Do you also have biographical amnesia?"

"I wish I did, man. I like you, King Arthur, you resonate, you're sending out good vibrations."

"Thank you, sir."

"You need to ditch those threads, man, sell that

crazy suit. I have just what you need."

Twenty minutes later Arthur stood silently in front of the mirror, assessing his brilliant tie-dyed tee shirt and bell-bottom jeans, earthy leather sandals.

"Perhaps I should seek employment as one of Barnum and Bailey's beloved clowns; that would indeed be a most curious turn of events." He stopped short. How did he know about Barnum and Bailey's clowns when he could not remember his own name?

"Now you have to grow your hair, man."

"I believe it shall grow quite nicely without my assistance."

"Whoa, I get that, man, you're not your hair, and your hair isn't you. That's deep. This body is an illusion, man. None of this is real, it's just a dream—and maybe it's not even *my* dream, maybe someone else is dreaming me."

"A most interesting proposition, sir." Arthur picked up his suit coat, feeling something in the inner pocket. He pulled out a small manilla envelope, opening it. There was a piece of woven fabric inside the envelope, a small note written in black ink beside it.

Found beneath the Temple
of the Feathered Serpent, 1883

Arthur carefully folded the envelope, slipping it into his pocket. For some unknown reason he knew this small piece of cloth was a vital clue to his past, and a secret which must never be revealed.

After several days, Arthur began feeling the urge to go outside, to explore this new environment. His new friend Sky agreed to accompany him, to roam the city with him.

As they strolled along the bustling sidewalks, Sky said, "We're aliens visiting a crazy new world, strangers in a strange land."

"My sentiments exactly, sir. I do feel quite like an alien disguised as a human in this strange world. These vehicles might well be alien ships from a far distant planet."

"Far out, sir, if I may say so."

Arthur laughed. He liked Sky, liked the way he said anything that came to his mind, not holding his thoughts and feelings captive inside him.

Arthur was learning a great deal about Sky during their excursions through the city, including the fact that Sky had been a third-year psychology major at Columbia University before he dropped out, deciding to find himself, discover who he really was and what his purpose was in this world. Unfortunately, he took a wrong turn along the way, experimenting with any number of psychedelic drugs, leading him down a disastrous path to the group home, unable to cope with the world as it was.

Arthur realized that in many ways their predicaments were quite similar, each of them trying to understand the true nature of their identity and their place in this world.

It was on one of these expeditions into the alien metropolis called New York, that Arthur spotted the old man. They had stopped to cross the street, Arthur noticing a lovely three-story home with its own driveway and private garage. There was a middle-aged woman raking leaves in the gated front yard. She smiled when she saw them, waving. “I love your shirts!”

Sky flashed her the peace sign as a thank-you, but Arthur’s eyes were on the face in the second story window, a white-haired man peering down at them, his eyes focused on Arthur, a chill running through him. Something was happening, but Arthur had no idea what. The man pulled the curtains closed, disappearing from view.

Arthur was still staring at the window when the streetlight changed, Sky heading across the street. “Let’s go, King Arthur, we must explore this vast and mysterious realm, rescuing the sleeping princess.”

Arthur laughed, enjoying Sky's humor; how he seemed to not have a care in the world. "Onward, sir, always onward."

Chapter 8

As they crossed the street, Arthur's thoughts were still on the man peering down at him from the second story window. Who was he? Why had he been looking at Arthur in such a fashion, so directly? Had he recognized him? Was it possible he knew who Arthur was? Was Arthur being guided by some unseen force to that house? Or was it all just his imagination? Perhaps he should return to the house. He considered this idea, but quickly realized it could have disastrous results. On the other hand, there was a chance the man would be able to identify him.

He turned to Sky as they strolled along. "Do you think there is a possibility that we are guided by unseen forces, directing us toward people and places which we need to see?"

"Of course it is, man. It happens every day, people just don't notice it. The thing is, those unseen forces are right here." He pressed one finger to his forehead. "We are the unseen forces, man."

Arthur nodded. Sky was an enigma, of that there was no doubt. There was far more depth to him than his outward appearance would first indicate. "Perhaps you are correct, sir. What you say does make sense."

"You're guided by your intuitive unconscious, that's the unseen force. You should read Carl Jung's book on synchronicity, man. It'll blow your mind."

"That name sounds vaguely familiar, although I have no idea where or when I heard it."

"He was a psychoanalyst, friends for a while with Freud, and one of the greatest minds to ever drop into this crazy world."

The following day Arthur returned to the house where he had seen the old man watching him.

He stood on the other side of the street, gazing up at the window, but the curtains were drawn. He could knock on the door, but what would he say? That he had biographical amnesia? That he thought the old man who looked out the window might know who he was? They would think him to be a madman, and perhaps they would be right. On the other hand, Sky had told him to pay close attention to the unseen forces that were guiding him, to listen to them, to act on them.

As he was watching the house, the front door opened, the woman he had seen raking the lawn the day before stepping out, a flower pot in one hand. She gazed at him curiously, then waved. "Love your shirt!"

Arthur crossed the street, a thought coming to him. He would not be meeting this woman if Sky had not given him the tie-dyed shirt. That was curious. He approached the gate, giving a friendly wave. She walked down the pathway, clearly trying to assess him.

"Your shirt is so colorful. Do you sell them?"

"My friend gave it to me. His name is Sky."

"He was the guy you were with before?"

Arthur said, "He was. I was wondering if perhaps you needed any help with your yard work? I've always thought I would be a good gardener, growing things, tending to them."

"What's your name?"

"I am Arthur. Sky calls me King Arthur because I don't know my last name."

"You don't know your last name?"

"I have what the doctors call biographical amnesia. They think it may have been caused by a traumatic event, but of course I have no memory of it."

"Where do you live, Arthur?"

"I am currently living in a group home in Brooklyn. Sky is my roommate."

"Do you know anything about gardening?"

"I am a quick learner and I think I would enjoy it, watching plants grow, taking care of them, nurturing them. I have no fear of hard work, if that is your concern."

The woman thought for a moment, then said, "I can pay you a dollar an hour to help out, take care of the yard, keep everything clean, tend to all the flowers, cut the lawn, do all the weeding. How does that sound? I can teach you about all the flowers, how to tend to them. How about we try it for a few days and see how it works out?"

"This is more than kind of you."

She looked at him curiously. "You said you're from Brooklyn?"

"I don't know where I am from. My last memory is of being in an alleyway in Brooklyn with a terrible headache, my face scraped badly from a fall."

"Do you think you were mugged?"

"The doctors said there were no physical injuries which would explain the amnesia."

"You don't sound like you're from Brooklyn, but I can't place your accent, the way you phrase things. It almost sounds old-fashioned, or kind of British, but you don't have a British accent. It sounds like how people used to talk way back when, much more formal."

Arthur nodded, deciding not to tell her about the old-fashioned suit he was wearing when the police found him.

The woman swung the iron gate open. “Come on in. My name is Clara Smith. My husband’s name is Albert. He’s away on business.”

Arthur worked at Mrs. Smith’s three or four days a week for the next four months, Clara teaching him everything she knew about gardening—about the rose bushes, the peonies, tulips, irises, delphiniums, and dahlias—telling him they each had their own individual personalities, their own needs. Some liked the sun, some the shade; some bloomed in the spring, some in late summer, some in the fall. He learned to clip the spent blossoms, called deadheading; how to prune the camellias and wisteria; how to water them; how to weed the garden beds. She taught him about dividing and replanting in the spring and fall, about mulching with bark and straw.

He was on his knees, weeding the dahlias, when he heard the front door open, footsteps on the porch. He looked up to see Clara carrying a pitcher of lemonade and two glasses, setting them down on a wicker table. She waved to him. “Arthur, take a break, it’s hot out, have some lemonade.”

Arthur got up, taking off his gardening gloves,

walking up the stairs to the front porch, Clara motioning for him to take a seat.

He pulled out a chair, sitting down, watching has she poured him a glass of lemonade, the ice clinking in the glass.

"You're doing such a marvelous job, Arthur. You really are a natural gardener. I've even gotten compliments from the neighbors on how nice the garden looks. I'd like to double your wages, pay you two dollars an hour."

"Thank you, I do appreciate your kind comments. Gardening does not feel like work to me. I find a hidden joy in it, although it is difficult to clearly define."

"You have not recovered any of your lost memories?"

"I have not. Perhaps a few tantalizing glimpses here and there, but nothing more. I have dreams of a young woman with orange hair, someone who I think was dear to me, but I don't know her name or if she is even real."

The front door of the house opened, an elderly white-haired man stepping out, a carved wooden cane in one hand. He walked over to the table, pulling out a chair, taking a seat, pouring himself a glass of lemonade. Arthur averted his eyes, afraid to make eye contact with the old man—the man who had been watching him from the second floor window.

The man looked at Arthur. "The garden looks lovely. Clara says you are doing a marvelous job."

Arthur forced himself to make eye contact. "Thank you, sir. That is most kind of you."

"Clara says you lost your memory. Is that true? You don't know who you are, where you came from?"

"She is correct. The doctors say I have biographical amnesia brought on by a traumatic event."

"That's what they say, is it?"

"It is."

"What do you think about that?"

"I don't quite understand the question, sir."

"Do you think you experienced a traumatic event? Something you're trying to forget?"

"I do not recall such an event. I wish it were otherwise; I wish I could remember if I had a family or friends."

"Perhaps one day you shall. Clara says you have a friend named Sky. That's an odd name."

"It is a name he has chosen for himself. I do not know his true name."

The old man leaned back in his chair. "A rose by any other name would smell as sweet."

Arthur furrowed his brow. He had heard that before, but he had no idea where.

The old man said, "Shakespeare, Romeo and Juliet. You're always you, no matter what anyone calls you."

"That is quite true, sir. Sky has said something along similar lines."

The man reached into his jacket pocket, pulling something out, setting it down on the wicker table, studying Arthur's face. It was a small stone carving, a figurine.

A single word popped out of Arthur's mouth. Unfortunately he had no idea what it meant.

"Tláloc."

The man picked up the figurine, putting it back in his pocket. He rose up, grabbing his cane, stopping when he was standing next to Arthur. He rested his hand on Arthur's shoulder for a moment, saying, "I pray that your memory returns, young man. I am truly sorry."

Clara watched as her father stepped back into the house, a look of concern on her face.

Arthur said, "Is your father well?"

"I don't know. That was odd, I don't know why he did that, said that. I hate to see him getting old."

"Why did he show me the stone figurine?"

"I don't know. Sometimes he does odd things like that. When you saw it, you said something. What did it mean?"

"I have no idea the meaning of the word, it just unexpectedly came out of my mouth."

Clara laughed. "The two of you make a fine pair. I hope your memories come back to you. To be honest, I'm dying to know where you're from."

It was a warm Saturday afternoon that found Arthur and Sky walking along Moore Street, on their way back to the group home.

Arthur said, "Do you ever consider returning to your studies in psychology at Columbia University?"

Sky stopped, his eyes on Arthur. "Are you one of Carl Jung's synchronistic events, a metaphorical archetype, a man with no idea who he is, telling me that I have discovered who I am?"

"I don't know what I am. What do you think I am?"

"You're a young King Arthur, on a quest to find Camelot, to find his home, to find his princess, find his castle."

A spontaneous idea popped into Arthur's head. It just felt like the right thing to do. He stood up, turning to Sky.

"You have proven yourself to be brave and loyal. It is time that you become a Knight of the Realm. Kneel down, if you would."

Sky kneeled down, bowing his head.

Arthur touched his shoulder. “From this day forth, you shall be known to all in the land as Sir Sky, a brave and loyal Knight of the Realm. You may rise, Sir Sky.”

Sir Sky stood up, his eyes on Arthur. “You have honored me, King Arthur. I vow from this day forth to protect the innocent, showing mercy to all, offering aid to those in need.”

Arthur had a feeling that something in Sky had changed. He was most certainly taking his knighthood to heart.

Two days later, as they were sitting on the grass in Central Park, Arthur leaning back against a tree, Sir Sky said. “I have been thinking a great deal, King Arthur, and I have realized there is something I must do. I am proud to be a brave and loyal Knight of the Realm, but the time has come for me to leave Camelot behind me, returning to my homeland to battle the fearsome dragons surrounding my castle. I have waited long enough.”

Arthur studied Sky’s face. “What fearsome dragons will you battle, Sir Sky? Do they have names?”

Sir Sky nodded, then said, “They do. My father was an alcoholic. Sometimes he was nice, sometimes he would come home drunk and beat my mother.”

Arthur knew the game had ended. “I’m sorry. No

child should have to face such things."

"When I was ten I tried to stop him from hitting her and he pushed me down the stairs, broke my leg. The next day he cried, apologizing, promising he would never drink again, never hit my mother again, never hurt me again."

"Did he keep his promise?"

"He did not. Three months later I came home from school and found him in the kitchen. He'd shot himself. There was an empty vodka bottle on the floor, a half-made sandwich on the counter, an open jar of mayonnaise, an empty can of tunafish. Right in the middle of making a sandwich he decided to kill himself. I remember putting the lid back on the jar of mayonnaise, putting it back in the refrigerator so it wouldn't go bad. I didn't know what else to do."

Arthur was silent.

"I always felt it was my fault, that I could have done something; been nicer to him, been funnier, gotten better grades, done something to make him want to keep living, anything. I should have been able to help him. He was my father."

"You were a child, that was not your job, sir."

"I sat in the kitchen until my mom got home. I kept thinking maybe he would wake up. I didn't want anyone else to know what he'd done. I didn't want to tell my friends what I had seen."

"What happened after that? After your father was gone?"

"My mom fell apart for a while, cried a lot, hugged me a lot, then remarried a year later to a nice guy. She had told everyone my father had run off with another woman. It was easier that way. Life went on. I tried to forget, pretend it had never happened, but I couldn't forget it—I couldn't forget putting that jar of mayonnaise in the refrigerator."

Arthur said, "Such wounds do not heal with time."

Sky nodded. "True. It's why I became a psych major. I was trying to fix him, trying to fix myself. I know that now."

Arthur pointed to a smashed beer bottle next to a large rock. "Can you fix that bottle? Make it whole again?"

Sky shook his head. "No."

"Some things can be fixed, and some things cannot be fixed, no matter how hard we try." He blinked when an image of the girl with orange hair flashed through his thoughts. He continued, "You said the unseen forces within us are there to guide us. They draw people and events to us without us being aware. You said most people think such things are random events, that there is no rhyme or reason for them, believing them to be nothing more than the arbitrary twists and turns of fortune."

Sky was hunched forward, staring silently at the smashed beer bottle.

Arthur continued, "Can you think of a reason why fate might have forced you to experience such an unbearably painful event as the one you did?"

Sky was quiet for almost a minute, then said, "To truly understand what it feels like for a child to lose a parent to suicide, how helpless they feel, the guilt they feel, the anger, the unbearable loss." He turned slowly, his eyes on Arthur. "Why are you here, King Arthur? Who are you, really? I need to know."

"I don't know."

"I've never told that story to anyone before."

"Perhaps it was time, perhaps you were ready to tell it, and I was ready to listen."

Sky shook his head. "I don't think so. It seems like it's more than that—forces aligning, doors opening as if by magic, choirs of angels singing, clouds parting."

"What will you do now?"

"I need to think about it."

Several weeks passed, Sky finally disclosing to Arthur that his real name was Robert Foster, that he grew up in Brooklyn, that he was going back to Columbia University to get whatever psychology degrees he needed to become a counselor for children and teenagers who had experienced similar traumatic events.

Arthur said, “I will miss you, Sir Sky. You have helped me more than you shall ever know.”

“Thank you, King Arthur. I fear the dragons would have destroyed me if you had not appeared when you did. Always remember, you don’t need to know your name to know who you are.”

“You are quite right, a name is only a name.”

As Sky was turning to leave, he said, “Let those unseen forces guide you, King Arthur, and they will bring you safely home.”

“I shall do exactly that, sir.”

Sir Sky was gone, Arthur sitting alone in the room, contemplating his next move, the calendar on the wall declaring the year to be 1968. He never saw Sir Sky again.

Chapter 9

Arthur continued his daily explorations of the city, this time on his own, quite comfortable now with the New York City subway system, after his previous excursions with Sir Sky.

One day, on a whim which felt like more than a whim, he decided to pay a visit to Columbia University, thinking that perhaps it had been more than a coincidence that Sky was a student there.

He took the IRT Lexington Avenue Line to 14th Street-Union Square, then transferred to the 1 train at 14th Street, taking him straight to the Columbia campus.

Arthur stood silently, gazing at the stately university buildings, studying them for any clues as to why he was there. He calmed his mind, strolling across the campus, knowing he would not see Sir Sky here, that his purpose this day was something else entirely, although what that purpose was he had no idea.

He stopped for a time, sitting on a bench, taking in

his surroundings, watching the students stroll past, listening to them talking, laughing, enjoying the day. Perhaps he had his own dragons to slay here, and that was why he had met Sky. He turned slowly, stopping when his eyes landed on a three-story building with a distinctive stone and brick facade, the lower level constructed of white stone, the upper two floors of red brick. There was something curious about the building—it was as if he was seeing a vaguely familiar face in a crowd, uncertain if he knew them, or if they simply resembled someone he had once known.

He got up, walking toward the building, stopping in front of it, reading the plaque outside the entrance—a plaque which identified the building as The Faculty House of Columbia University. He felt himself being drawn to the building, stepping over to the entrance, as though retracing his own ghostly steps.

He entered through the front doors, no one raising an eyebrow at the sight of his colorful tie-dyed shirt, no one questioning his presence there. He walked up the stairs that led to the second floor, then continued up to the third floor, noting the long hallway, a dark green door at one end, unable to make out the words on it. He stepped down the hallway, reaching the door, reading the sign.

Pulling the door open, he made his way up the stairs into the dimly lit attic of the building, studying its dusty interior, the stacks of boxes and old furniture, the metal ductwork, copper piping, and electrical cables running across the rafters. He paused. Why was he here? Was he mad, imagining unseen forces guiding him? Perhaps so, perhaps not. He continued on, heading toward the far right corner of the shadowy room, feeling as though a hidden part of him was controlling his every movement.

When he reached the far corner, he kneeled down, picking up a rusty nail, using it to pry up one of the floorboards, revealing a dust-covered red leather pouch. He breathed a sigh of relief, reaching for the pouch. He was not mad after all—this was the reason he was here.

He picked it up, carefully loosening the leather drawstring, pulling the pouch open, peering into it. It was filled with at least twenty gold coins. He removed one of them, examining it. It was a Double Eagle twenty-dollar gold coin from 1907. There was a note inside the pouch, written in ink, the handwriting shaky, faded.

For dear Arthur, as he sets out on a grand and noble adventure. All our love, Grandma and Grandpa

A great sadness washed through him. He had no idea who his Grandma and Grandpa were, only that they had given him these gold coins. They must have loved him, and he must have loved them.

He spent the rest of the afternoon strolling around the campus, looking at the buildings, watching the students, trying to remember. He knew he had been here sometime in the past, hiding the gold coins in the Faculty House. This was curious, as he could not have been a faculty member since he was far too young, twenty years old at the most.

The unseen force that was guiding him—what Sir Sky had called his intuitive unconscious—had left him. He was on his own again, lost in this mysterious realm.

Despite his loneliness, he took comfort in the gold coins weighing heavily in his coat pocket. They were real, they were solid, and they were proof that he had been here before, that this world had been his home before he lost his memories. More importantly, they were proof that someone had loved him.

As the weeks passed, Arthur came to see that

although he had not discovered his old identity, he was creating a new one, possibly a better one. He also realized he would be able to live on his own now; able to leave the safety and security of the group home.

The gold coins he found in the Faculty House enabled him to do exactly that. As luck would have it, one of the coins proved to be extremely rare, an 1870 Carson City Liberty Head Double Eagle, Arthur selling the coin for almost three thousand dollars, a vast sum of money in 1968, and enough money for him to rent a room of his own for the modest sum of one hundred dollars per month.

His new landlord proved to be both courteous and honest, but someone who kept to himself, making an appearance just once a month to collect the rent.

Despite having enough funds to rent the room for several years, Arthur realized he needed to find employment, something that paid more than the seasonal gardening did. Unfortunately, he had no idea what other skills he might possess.

The day came when his explorations of the city brought him to the American Museum of Natural History on 79th Street, the building coming into view as he strolled aimlessly through Central Park, his thoughts on a recent dream about the girl with the orange hair.

He stopped when he saw the museum, eyeing the imposing structure, having the confidence now to trust his inner guidance system—a system which he believed was powered by the memories hidden within him. It had been almost a year now, his memories stubbornly refusing to reveal themselves.

He entered through the front doors of the museum, purchasing a day ticket, stepping into the cavernous entrance hall, gaping at the impossibly large skeleton of a prehistoric brontosaurus.

He said to no one in particular, "Good heavens, that creature's size is staggering."

The man standing next to him laughed. "You got that right, buddy. Wouldn't want to feed him every day, know what I'm saying?"

"I do indeed, sir. It would take a king's ransom to feed such a beast."

Arthur spent a good portion of the day strolling through the museum, fascinated by the displays, especially the immense skeletons of the prehistoric beasts, imagining what they must have looked like when they freely roamed the earth so many millions of years ago.

His wanderings eventually led him to the Hall of Mexico and Central America, the extraordinary displays showcasing a vast collection of artifacts from

Aztec, Mayan, Incan, and other pre-Columbian civilizations.

Arthur felt a wave of familiarity roll through him, along with the realization that this was why he was here. It was a most extraordinary feeling, and yet quite indescribable.

He strolled through the displays, chills running through him as he studied the myriad of Mesoamerican artifacts, each item carefully labeled. As he approached the large stone carving of a Mayan warrior-lord bearing weapons, he noticed a uniformed guard keeping a watchful eye on him. Perhaps it was his tie-dyed tee shirt which was drawing the guard's attention. The guard began to follow him as he slowly made his way through the exhibits.

Arthur paused when he noticed two small stone carvings in a glass display case which were not labeled, studying them. Surprising himself more than the guard, he turned to face the uniformed man, now standing only ten feet behind him. Arthur pointed to the two carvings, saying, "Xiuhcoatl the Fire Serpent, and Tepeyollotl, God of Earthquakes and Caves, from the Temple of the Feathered Serpent in Teotihuacan. They're not labelled. I just thought you should be aware of this, sir."

The guard stepped over to him. "Do you work

here?"

"I do not. I simply noticed that these two carvings were without identification and wished to inform you of their appropriate origins."

The guard stared at him, studying his colorful tee shirt, bell-bottom jeans, and leather sandals. Finally he blinked. "Wait here, I'll be right back."

"Of course."

It happened as Arthur was watching the guard walk away. He grabbed one of the display cases, trying to steady himself, the ground beneath him shaking, the air shimmering with a green mist, a flood of ten thousand names and dates and places pouring into him, filling him with a sudden astonishing knowledge of Mesoamerican civilizations. He leaned over, afraid he might faint, Sir Sky's last words reverberating in his thoughts. *"Let those unseen forces guide you, King Arthur, and they will bring you safely home."*

It was true, it was all true.

Ten minutes later an elderly man in a gray suit and tie approached him with a pleasant, disarming smile, Arthur having recovered from the extraordinary event.

"Good afternoon, young man, I am Dr. Fernald, a curator here at the museum. One of the guards said you might have some information regarding two unlabelled artifacts?"

Arthur pointed to the two carved figures. "Xiuhcoatl the Fire Serpent, and Tepeyollotl, God of Earthquakes and Caves, from the Temple of the Feathered Serpent in Teotihuacan."

The curator took a step back, a look of distinct surprise on his face. "May I ask how you came to acquire such knowledge? You don't look old enough to have studied at university."

"If I could answer you, I would, sir. But I'm afraid I am suffering from what is known as biographical amnesia, perhaps the result of an unknown traumatic event."

"I have never encountered such a thing. You are quite serious about this?"

"Quite serious, indeed, sir."

"How is it you are able to identify the carvings, and yet unable to remember your identity?"

"To be quite honest, when I entered the Hall of Mexico and Central America, the memories of these artifacts—the names, dates, and places—came flooding back to me. It is most astonishing, and I have no explanation for what has happened."

"May I ask you some questions, testing your knowledge of these artifacts? It's all quite extraordinary, and most intriguing."

"Of course you may."

For almost an hour they strolled through the exhibits, the curator asking endless questions about the displays, about Mesoamerican civilizations, only two or three of the questions stumping Arthur.

Finally, Dr. Fernald said, "I have seen enough to know you are the genuine article; your knowledge of Mesoamerican civilizations is quite extraordinary, especially for someone as young as yourself. May I inquire as to your current employment status?"

"I am currently without employment, due in great part to my case of amnesia."

"It is indeed most curious. Would you be interested in a position as a research assistant here at the museum? The pay is quite good, as are the hours."

Arthur did not hesitate. "I can think of nothing I would enjoy more, sir."

"It's settled then, all we need to do is fill out the paperwork."

"My first name is Arthur, but I can't tell you my last name. It is lost to me."

"We shall call you Arthur Doe, then. I think that should suffice for the time being. As you mentioned, there is a good chance your memories shall return to you, and perhaps spending time around these artifacts will stir those forgotten memories. Might I politely, and without judgement of any kind, suggest a change of wardrobe, perhaps something slightly less colorful?"

Arthur laughed. "Of course, sir. I believe my invaluable excursion into the colorful world of tie-dyed garments has come to a close."

Arthur was thrilled with his new position at the museum, becoming somewhat of a celebrity—the young man with amnesia who had an almost encyclopedic knowledge of Mesoamerican civilizations. There was even an article in the New York Times about him; a number of celebrity psychics suggesting young Arthur Doe was possessed by the spirit of a long-dead anthropologist, or that he was the reincarnation of a long-dead anthropologist, or that he was channeling the thoughts of a long-dead anthropologist.

Either way, Arthur took it all in stride, enjoying these fleeting moments of fame, knowing it would soon pass, that people's attention would move on to something else, some other shiny new distraction.

For over two years he worked at the museum, rising in rank, becoming a well-respected expert on Mesoamerican cultures, getting a number of raises which allowed him to move to more substantial lodgings. With help from Dr. Fernald and the administrators at the museum, he was able to obtain a social security number and a New York City identification card, after numerous attempts to discover his former identity had proven unsuccessful.

Three years had passed since he had taken the position at the museum, Arthur finally feeling at home in the great city of New York, taking the subway to work every day, acquiring numerous new friends and acquaintances, being well-liked by all who knew him.

Despite all of his success, all of his accolades, his memories had not returned to him. When he lay in bed at night, as he was drifting off to sleep, he was still plagued by a profound sense of homesickness, of loss, haunted by something which was missing, something he could not identify. His dreams about the young woman with orange hair were occurring more often.

He had seen her in a dream only a few nights ago. She was standing in front of The Temple of the Feathered Serpent, dressed in khaki clothing, smiling at him, but he had no idea what that meant. He suspected his dream was mingling his world at the museum with memories of his past. Although at times he suspected she existed only in his dreams, he still found himself unconsciously scanning the passengers on the subway, searching for this phantom woman, searching for the woman with the bright orange hair.

Everything changed in an instant on a chilly morning in early November. Arthur was bundled up in a long dark woolen coat, making his way to the subway station, thinking of nothing but the unfinished tasks which lay ahead of him at the museum, when he heard a curious, but strangely familiar, crunching sound coming from the construction site he was walking past. He stopped, listening to the sound.

When he turned toward it, he saw a man wearing rough khaki clothing digging in the ground with a long-handled shovel—the source of the oddly familiar crunching sound, the steel shovel clashing against rocks and earth. He studied the man, filled with an almost unearthly chill.

It was happening again. The ground seemed to tremble, the air shimmering, the world taking on a strange green tint. He felt faint, grabbing onto a parking meter to steady himself. That was the singular moment when Arthur remembered everything. He knew who he was, where he came from, and how he came to be in New York City in the year 1968. He also knew the name of the girl with the bright orange hair.

Chapter 10

"Losing your way on a journey is unfortunate. But, losing your reason for the journey is a fate more than cruel." — *H.G. Wells*

The Temple of the Feathered Serpent

April 4, 1910 was a gloriously sunny spring day, a Monday, and a day that found young Miss Bristol strolling across the Columbia University campus toward its esteemed Department of Anthropology, located in Schermerhorn Hall. Miss Bristol was brimming with confidence on that day, almost buoyant, smartly dressed in a crisp white blouse with a high laced collar, a black satin bow tie, and a long, slightly flared skirt hiding her sturdy lace-up boots. She was undeniably a striking figure, with her bright orange hair, and the only female research assistant in the anthropology department. She was extremely proud of her current position, both expecting and receiving precisely the same treatment as her male counterparts, with no exceptions.

Stepping past Romanesque stone pillars into Schermerhorn Hall, she strolled toward the main office of the anthropology department, her footsteps echoing down the long hallway. A young man tipped his hat to her as he was passing, saying, "Good morning, Miss Bristol. A lovely day, is it not?"

She nodded to him politely, replying, "It is indeed, sir. I believe April to be the loveliest month of the year."

"As do I, Miss Bristol."

She arrived at the main office, pulling open the heavy oaken door, stepping inside, presenting a bright smile to the rather stern-faced woman seated at an oversized oaken desk, her gray hair wrapped in an exceedingly tight bun.

Miss Bristol said, "Good morning, Mrs. Fletcher. I trust your day is going well?"

"Quite well, indeed, Miss Bristol. It is an unusual request, but Professor Hollingsworth has left a note saying he would like to see you in his office the moment you arrive."

"Whatever for, Mrs. Fletcher?"

"He gave me no reason, Miss Bristol, only that he wished to see you as soon as you arrive."

"Very well, I shall go there directly. I do not wish to keep the professor waiting."

She stepped out into the hallway, striding toward her destination, a look of some concern on her face. Mrs. Fletcher was quite correct, this was an unusual request from Professor Hollingsworth, and a slightly worrisome one. Perhaps she had made an error when cataloguing the Mayan artifacts and he was displeased with her. This was a most unsettling thought for Miss Bristol. Less than a minute later she stood before a gleaming brass plaque mounted on an ornately carved office door.

Professor Arthur B. Hollingsworth
Department of Anthropology

She knocked soundly on the door, a voice calling out, "Enter!"

Miss Bristol opened the door, entering the professor's office, giving a brief but curious glance at the man standing in front of Professor Hollingsworth's desk, a man she did not recognize.

"Good morning, Miss Bristol. You are punctual as always, a most admirable quality."

"Thank you, Professor Hollingsworth. Mrs. Fletcher said you wished to see me as soon as I arrived?"

"Quite true, quite true." He leaned back in his chair, studying Miss Bristol, then the unknown visitor, as if assessing their current states of mind. He looked at Miss Bristol. "I trust you are having a pleasant day, enjoying our marvelous April weather?"

"I am indeed, sir. It is a lovely day." Miss Bristol gave an internal sigh of relief—clearly this had nothing to do with her performance as a research assistant. But she also had to restrain herself from asking him the purpose of her visit, and more importantly, the identity of the unknown man standing next to her.

"Miss Bristol, I should like to introduce to you Professor George Wexley of the physics department, a brilliant and highly regarded physicist. Professor Wexley, this is one of our most dedicated and knowledgable research assistants, Miss Bristol. I should forewarn you, do not be misled by her gender; Miss Bristol is a brilliant mind."

Professor Wexley nodded to her, tipping his hat. "A great pleasure to meet you, Miss Bristol. You are indeed a notable rarity, a female research assistant at Columbia, a college which does not accept female students."

Miss Bristol nodded in return. “Perhaps I shall help to remedy that situation, sir. The world is changing.”

“It is indeed, Miss Bristol, and I wish you the best in your endeavors.”

“It is a pleasure to meet you, sir, although I am quite curious as to the reason why we have both been called here so early in the morning.”

Professor Wexley laughed. “As am I, Miss Bristol, most curious indeed. It is not often that a professor of physics is called to the Department of Anthropology.”

Professor Hollingsworth rose to his feet. “All will become clear shortly. A rather peculiar situation has arisen over the last few weeks, one which I feel compelled to share with both of you, but one which demands the utmost confidentiality on your parts. Not a word of what I shall tell you must leave this room. Can both of you agree to this caveat?”

Professor Wexley said, “You have piqued my curiosity no end, sir. I readily agree to your condition.”

Miss Bristol nodded. “As do I.”

“Miss Bristol, may I ask you, have you ever heard of a man by the name of Desiré Charnay?”

“Of course, sir, he was the French archeologist who frequented Mesoamerican ruins in the late 1800s, particularly those at Teotihuacan, and more specifically the Temple of the Feathered Serpent.”

Professor Wexley said, "I'm afraid you have lost me, Miss Bristol. I am quite unfamiliar with any of those locations."

Professor Hollingsworth nodded. "That is quite understandable, sir. Miss Bristol is correct, however. Charnay was a French anthropologist who studied the ancient civilizations of Mexico and Central America. He was the impetus behind the formation of a notable 1883 expedition to Teotihuacan—a most remarkable ancient ruins in central Mexico—Charnay returning with a great number of highly significant artifacts."

"That is most interesting, but I'm afraid I still do not understand the reason for my presence here, Professor."

"Quite so. Something Miss Bristol is not aware of, I am quite certain, is that a member of Desiré Charnay's 1883 expedition was a student of anthropology named Frederick Beaumont, at that time a research assistant at Columbia University's Department of Anthropology." He raised his eyebrows knowingly.

Professor Wexley and Miss Bristol were silent, their eyes on Professor Hollingsworth, waiting for him to continue.

"Mr. Beaumont returned to Columbia with two wooden crates filled with lesser artifacts, none comparable to those brought back by Charnay, of course"

Silence again echoed through the room.

"Recently, I came across those same two crates in storage. I discovered them in a dusty corner of the basement, more than likely untouched since their return in 1883."

Professor Wexley shifted his weight from one foot to the other, giving an audible sigh.

Professor Hollingsworth held up one finger. "Patience, sir. You are about to learn the reason for your presence here."

Miss Bristol bit her lip, trying not to smile.

"I searched through the contents of both wooden crates, looking for anything which might have been overlooked, and indeed I found something quite unexpected, quite extraordinary, and most notably, the reason for Professor Wexley's presence here today." He paused dramatically.

"Great heavens, sir, I am begging you, please disclose the reason for my presence before I die of old age."

Miss Bristol burst out laughing, covering her mouth with one hand. "I beg your pardon, Professor."

Professor Hollingsworth smiled, obviously enjoying himself. "I found an object tucked into a rather ordinary small clay pot, along with a note stating precisely where the object had been found—in a hidden tunnel deep beneath the Temple of the Feathered Serpent." He reached into his coat pocket, pulling out a six-inch long sleeve of pale gray woven fabric, dropping it onto the desk with a flourish, taking a step back, awaiting their response.

Professor Wexley frowned. "I am at a loss for words, sir. To be quite forthcoming, I fear you may have taken leave of your senses."

"Humor me, if you will, Professor. Pick up the fabric, feel it."

With a sigh, Professor Wexley reached over and plucked the fabric from the desk, holding it in his hands. "You are quite correct, it is indeed fabric. May I take my leave, sir?"

"Stretch the fabric, if you would, sir."

Wexley pulled on the fabric, stretching it. "It is truly fantastic, a fabric that stretches. We are indeed living in the age of modern miracles. Will that be all, sir?"

"Stretch it more, sir."

Wexley stretched it out to arm's length, a look of curiosity appearing on his face. "This is rather remarkable, it has stretched to at least eight times its original length."

Professor Hollingsworth said, "Miss Bristol, if you would be so kind as to take one end of the fabric, while Professor Wexley holds the other end, and walk over to the door?"

Professor Wexley's eyes widened when the fabric easily stretched over fourteen feet to the office door. "This is most curious, sir. I am at a loss as to how a fabric could do this."

"I have personally tested the fabric, attempting to determine precisely how far it is capable of stretching."

"What are the limits, sir? I am most curious."

"There are none that I can determine. I stretched it to well over a hundred feet with ease, quite certain I could have walked another mile without difficulty."

"This is quite impossible. I noted that when the fabric stretches, it does not lose any of its thickness. When one stretches a rubber band, it becomes thin, almost transparent, its mass remaining constant, but such is not the case with this fabric."

"It stretches both lengthwise and widthwise. If there were four of us and we each took a corner, it would easily stretch to the size of this room, a rectangular shape of twenty-two feet by twenty feet."

"I am astonished, sir. The fabric appears to be breaking the known laws of physics, gaining mass as it stretches out, and losing mass when released, quickly returning to its original form. I can see clearly now why you requested my presence, and I humbly apologize for both my impertinence and my impatience."

Professor Hollingsworth smiled. "You are quite forgiven, sir. There is more to this story, however—a great deal more."

Professor Hollingsworth picked up the mysterious sleeve of fabric, sliding it onto his arm, stretching it from his wrist to his shoulder, then reached into a desk drawer, pulling out a rather deadly looking jeweled dagger, its razor-sharp gleaming silver blade over eight inches long. "A souvenir from a rather perilous expedition into the mountains of Peru."

He handed the dagger to Professor Wexley, saying, "If you would be so kind as to stab my arm with the dagger?" He extended his sleeved arm to the professor.

"Good heavens, sir, you ask too much of me. I shall not stab your arm with this dagger. You have crossed a line, sir."

"Very well." Professor Hollingsworth took the dagger back, taking a seat at his desk, resting his sleeved arm across it, the dagger in his other hand.

Miss Bristol let out a cry when the professor raised the dagger above his head, bringing it down suddenly with full force, the blade of the dagger striking his arm directly. Miss Bristol turned away; she could not bear to see what happened.

In fact, nothing happened, the dagger stopping as if it had been confronted with a solid block of steel.

Professor Hollingsworth set the dagger down, removing the sleeve from his arm. "Not a scratch, and I felt nothing, not the slightest glimmer of pressure. The fabric did two things: it became impenetrable, and it absorbed all the energy of the dagger's strike."

Professor Wexley was pacing back and forth, his eyes on the fabric. "This is fantastic, impossible, and yet I have witnessed it with my own eyes."

Professor Hollingsworth said, "There is one more demonstration I should like to share with you, a rather theatrical one, but one you shall not soon forget." He stepped behind his desk, leaning down, lifting up a large orange pumpkin, placing it on the desktop. Picking up the cloth sleeve, he pulled it over the pumpkin, covering it.

"You are going to use the dagger on the pumpkin?"

"Better than that, sir." Professor Hollingsworth once again reached into his desk drawer, this time pulling out a heavy black revolver, holding it up for them to see. "This is a Webley Mark IV revolver, .455 caliber, an extremely reliable weapon currently in use by the British armed forces."

Miss Bristol took a step back. "Surely you do not intend to fire that weapon in this office."

"I absolutely intend to do that, Miss Bristol. It would be best if you both covered your ears."

Professor Wexley stepped back, attempting to increase the distance between himself and the revolver as rapidly as possible, his hands pressed against his ears.

Professor Hollingsworth raised the pistol and fired it directly at the pumpkin, the gun roaring, flames and smoke shooting out from the barrel, the room suddenly filled with the pungent odor of sulfur dioxide.

Miss Bristol's eyes had not left the pumpkin, watching as the heavy .455 caliber lead bullet collided with the mysterious fabric, the bullet stopping abruptly, falling harmlessly with a soft thud onto the desk.

Professor Hollingsworth reached over and picked up the heavy lead bullet. "You were in no danger at any time, I assure you. I have performed this test at least a dozen times before, each time with the same result—the bullet and the pumpkin remain unscathed, not a dent, not a scratch on either of them. The fabric sleeve completely absorbs the energy of the bullet."

The office door suddenly flew open, a wide-eyed man with an enormous mustache and bowler hat rushing in. "Was that a gunshot? Is anyone hurt? Do we need a doctor?"

Professor Hollingsworth said, "My apologies, I should have forewarned you. I fired a blank cartridge, a demonstration for our visiting physics professor. No harm done, it will not happen again."

The man glared at Professor Hollingsworth. "It will most certainly not happen again or you will face the most dire of consequences, Professor Hollingsworth. As you may well imagine, the whole floor is in a turmoil after hearing a gunshot."

"My deepest apologies, sir. I regret my decision to fire the weapon, and you have my solemn promise it will never happen again."

The man gave a loud sniff, glaring at the professor as he exited the room, closing the door forcefully behind him. Professor Hollingsworth winked at Miss Bristol, grinning.

Professor Wexley pulled the fabric from the pumpkin, examining it closely.

"If I had not witnessed it, I would not have believed it possible. I must think about this for a moment. Firstly, the fabric appears to be creating matter as it stretches, increasing its mass. This goes against all the known laws of physics, especially considering Professor Einstein's 1905 Special Relativity Theory where he proposes that $E = mc^2$. Simply put, he posits that mass and energy are interchangeable. Matter is nothing more than highly concentrated energy. The amount of energy it would take to create matter, to increase the volume of this fabric is astronomical. It is simply not possible. That being said, it is happening, so where can that energy possibly be coming from?

"Secondly, when struck with a dagger or a bullet, the fabric does not appear to be rapidly changing its form, becoming an impenetrable material, but more elegantly, it simply absorbs all the kinetic energy of the moving projectile. The question is, where does that energy go?"

Hollingsworth nodded. "You have summed it up quite succinctly, sir. There is another question, perhaps the most important one, which remains unanswered. Who created the fabric?"

Chapter 11

"Dare I say it, sir? I can reach no other conclusion save that your mysterious fabric is not of this world. It is infinitely beyond anything we are currently capable of creating."

Miss Bristol looked notably dubious. "You are suggesting the fabric comes from another world, some distant civilization? I fear you are lending far too much credence to the fantastical otherworldly tales of writers such as H.G. Wells and Jules Verne."

"Are you aware that Percival Lowell, a noted astronomer, has discovered canals on Mars, possible evidence suggesting the existence of intelligent life on the red planet?"

"I am still quite dubious; there must be a simpler explanation."

Professor Hollingsworth nodded his agreement. "Occam's Razor states that the simplest explanation is usually the correct one."

Professor Wexley shook his head. "I do not think

Occam's Razor applies to this particular case. The universe is incomprehensibly large, perhaps infinitely large, with no end to it, as some astronomers have suggested. Our own Milky Way galaxy contains as many as three or four hundred billion stars, and it is estimated there are at least two hundred billion other galaxies, many far larger than the Milky Way. Each of the stars in those galaxies is likely being orbited by planets such as ours. What are the odds that our little world is the only one in this infinite expanse where intelligent life is to be found?"

Miss Bristol furrowed her brow. "You make a salient point, Professor Wexley. Perhaps the stories written by Mr. Wells and his contemporaries are not so fanciful after all."

Hollingsworth said, "It is a most convincing argument, sir. If you are correct, and I suspect you are, it does not readily explain the presence of this fabric in our world."

Miss Bristol said, "Professor, you said there was a note left by Frederick Beaumont detailing precisely where the fabric was found?"

The two men turned toward Miss Bristol, a look of sudden clarity appearing on Professor Wexley's face. "You are quite brilliant indeed, Miss Bristol. You are saying we must return to the original source of the fabric, return to the secret tunnel beneath the Temple of… of…something with feathers, was it?"

Miss Bristol laughed. "You are close, sir. It was The Temple of the Feathered Serpent."

Hollingsworth slapped the desktop. "Exactly what I was going to suggest. Who knows what else we shall find there? I hereby propose an archeological expedition to Teotihuacan, the three of us exploring Beaumont's tunnel, deep beneath the Temple of the Feathered Serpent."

Professor Wexley said, "I accept your proposal most enthusiastically. We shall need, however, a ready explanation as to why a professor of physics would be accompanying you on an archeological excursion."

Miss Bristol shrugged. "Many people travel to distant lands simply to see the sights, nothing more. Perhaps such a trip might prove to be most enjoyable for you."

The professor laughed. "I believe it would, Miss Bristol. I foresee a much needed vacation when this spring semester comes to an end, perhaps a lovely voyage to the warm and sunny climes of Mexico. I hear they have some marvelous ancient ruins there, well worth visiting. I shall be certain to bring my camera."

Professor Hollingsworth rubbed his hands together. “It is settled then, we shall leave at the end of this semester, traveling to Teotihuacan to discover the source of this miraculous and infinitely confounding otherworldly fabric.”

“Well said, sir.”

“May I remind you again that we must reveal to no one the true purpose of this proposed expedition?”

“Of course.”

Professor Wexley picked up the fabric, studying it. “I hesitate to mention it, but I shall say it nonetheless. This fabric could make us all inconceivably wealthy. It could be used for an infinite variety of purposes; protective armor for soldiers, for example—they would be impervious to the enemies’ bullets.”

Miss Bristol added, “It could be stretched over a building, or even a city, protecting it from falling bombs dropped by a dirigible, or one of those new flying aeroplanes.”

Hollingsworth said, “You are both quite correct, but our primary goal at the present time is one of discovery—the advancement of scientific knowledge—not the attainment of personal wealth.”

Professor Wexley shrugged. “There is no reason why it could not satisfy both purposes, sir. Look at men like Edison, Bell, Ford, Marconi, and a dozen others. They have advanced science while simultaneously becoming wealthy men."

"You make a sound argument, sir. That being said, we will have to do a great deal more research and experimentation before determining if it is possible to duplicate the fabric using our current scientific technologies."

"Quite true, it is a pointless venture if we are unable to manufacture the fabric."

Miss Bristol said, "Perhaps we shall discover something in Teotihuacan that will resolve this issue."

After Professor Wexley had left, Professor Hollingsworth stood next to Miss Bristol, gazing out the window at the bright blue sky.

"Miss Bristol, I shall confess to you that after listening to Professor Wexley, it has become quite clear to me that the fabric came from a distant world, from beyond the stars. The question remains: who, or what, carried the fabric with them to our little planet?"

Miss Bristol shivered, uncertain whether she wanted to discover the answer to Professor Hollingsworth's question.

With the end of the spring semester only months away, Professor Hollingsworth, Miss Bristol, and Professor Wexley began preparations for their impending expedition to Teotihuacan.

Professor Hollingsworth would be responsible for arranging financial backing for their expedition, speaking at great length with Dr. Boas, the highly regarded head of the Anthropology Department at Columbia, and the man who would later become known as the father of American archeology.

After asking Professor Hollingsworth numerous pointed questions regarding the purpose of the expedition, Dr. Boas finally agreed that the school would finance the venture, albeit with certain stringent caveats which were then conveyed in detail to Miss Bristol by Professor Hollingsworth.

Professor Hollingsworth was also responsible for procuring the lengthy list of equipment and supplies they would need for the expedition: large canvas tents, ground cloths, folding cots and chairs, carbide lamps, and expedition wear—including hats, gaiters, boots, gloves and khaki clothing. They would also need an assortment of digging implements, including: shovels, spades, pickaxes, sieves, and soft bristle brushes, plus whatever other articles Professor Hollingsworth deemed necessary to ensure a successful expedition—items such as maps, journals, wooden packing crates, and survey equipment.

It was Miss Bristol's responsibility to make their travel arrangements, a challenging endeavor, but one she attacked with her usual unflagging vigor and determination.

Three weeks later, after visiting numerous steamship booking offices, railway line offices, and the Thomas Cook & Son Travel Agency in New York, Miss Bristol had finalized their travel plans, including the hiring of a foreman and ten laborers for the dig.

They would leave New York Harbor on June 4, departing from Pier 14 on the East River, traveling aboard the Ward Line's *SS Merida*, a sturdy, proven steamship of the New York and Cuba Mail Steamship Company. The ship would make a one-day stop in sunny Havana before continuing on to the bustling port city of Veracruz, Mexico, the journey taking a minimum of seven days, depending on weather conditions.

Their accommodations aboard the *SS Merida* would be second-class, not first-class, Dr. Boas having made it abundantly clear that they were not on a luxurious pleasure cruise, but on a scholarly archeological expedition. They would travel second-class or the university would not fund the expedition.

Upon disembarking in Veracruz, they would spend one night in a hotel, and the following day board the National Railways of Mexico passenger train which would carry them onward to Mexico City. Once again, following Dr. Boas' inflexible caveats, they would have second-class seats aboard the train, a twelve hour journey at minimum.

Despite this, Miss Bristol was quite looking forward to the train ride, this being the first time she had visited Mexico. She had at first been somewhat tentative about the seagoing segment of their journey, having never sailed on the open ocean, but decided to take a positive approach, seeing it as a grand adventure, and one which would undoubtedly help her to attain the ultimate prize, the acceptance of women as undergraduate students at Columbia College.

After their arrival in Mexico City, there would be another night in a hotel, and the following day, a four-hour horse-drawn carriage ride to Teotihuacan. If all went according to plan, their supplies would be waiting for them there, the canvas expedition tents already erected by the foreman she had hired to supervise the ten laborers who would be doing the digging.

Miss Bristol was eagerly anticipating their departure, telling Professor Hollingsworth that it would be the expedition of a lifetime. His reply had surprised her, and pleased her greatly.

"I believe it shall be the first of many archeological expeditions in your lifetime, Miss Bristol. You have proven quite invaluable to the department, and although it is not yet possible for you to receive an undergraduate degree from the college, I foresee a long and distinguished career in anthropology for you. As you said, times are changing, and the day will come when you shall have your degree. I am certain of it."

Miss Bristol smiled as she set down her pen. Professor Hollingsworth was a brilliant anthropologist, but he was also a kind and thoughtful man, a man of good nature, and one possessing an endless abundance of enthusiasm. She was quite fond of him, but of course she would keep such personal feelings to herself—any outward display of such thoughts would be monstrously inappropriate, bringing disgrace to the department and more than likely an end to Professor Hollingsworth's burgeoning academic career at the university. This was his first year as a full professor, having risen quickly through the ranks of assistant professor and associate professor.

It was Professor Wexley's task to delve into the puzzling physical characteristics of the strange fabric, attempting to discover the physical laws and mechanisms which would account for its seemingly impossible behavior. After dedicating three weeks to the task, he brought his inquiries to a sudden and most unsatisfying conclusion. He could find nothing in the current known laws of physics which would allow the fabric to do what he had seen it do. Science would have to delve far deeper into the perplexing relationship between physical matter and energy before they would be able to understand the underlying systems hidden within the fabric's molecular and subatomic structure which allowed it to so readily change its mass.

He was well aware of Max Planck's new theory that energy is composed of discreet segments he called quanta, and that Albert Einstein had proposed that light itself was composed of quanta, but for now, these were only abstract ideas, no one quite sure where such theories would take them. It would take decades, perhaps centuries, or even millennia, to fully reveal the universe's vast trove of unfathomable secrets.

At long last, the day of their eagerly anticipated departure for Teotihuacan arrived.

On the morning of June 4, 1910, Miss Bristol arrived in a horse-drawn carriage at the main gates of Pier 14 on the East River, the location agreed upon by the three adventurers as their meeting place.

Miss Bristol gazed at the teeming crowds of people gathered at the pier: dozens of porters handling luggage, vendors selling all manner of culinary delights and souvenirs, excited travelers and their families and friends who had come to see them off, and any number of uniformed crew members busily preparing the *SS Merida* for its impending departure.

Miss Bristol spotted Professor Hollingsworth and Professor Wexley standing next to the main gate, in the midst of conversation. She headed over to them, calling out and waving.

Professor Hollingsworth waved back. "There you are, Miss Bristol! How was your carriage ride? Have you ever seen such a crowd of people in one place?"

"It is marvelous, and I am thrilled beyond measure to be here. The ship is enormous, I was not expecting it to be so large."

"It is indeed large; almost four hundred feet long. We should check in, so the porters may take our steamer trunks."

They followed the clearly marked signs to the second-class embarkation area, showing their passports and answering a number of health related questions, the agents carefully scrutinizing all travelers in an attempt to identify anyone who might be carrying an infectious disease.

When Professor Hollingsworth confessed to the attendant that his laugh was quite infectious, the attendant gave him a severe look, a dark frown. Miss

Bristol stifled a laugh, covering her mouth with one hand.

With their steamer trunks checked in and on the way to the ship's cavernous cargo hold, the three companions headed up the gangway to the main deck of the ship, making their way through the lively throng of passengers to the port side of the vessel. Miss Bristol marveled that she could still see New York's majestic Singer Building, currently the tallest building in the world, standing at a staggering six hundred and twelve feet tall.

Professor Hollingsworth said, "Perhaps we should locate our cabins before the ship departs. We must follow the signs, keeping clear of the designated first-class areas. I should hate to be thrown overboard by an irate first-class passenger and be devoured by sharks."

Miss Bristol laughed. "Even worse than the sharks, you would miss out on the remarkable discoveries we shall make at The Temple of the Feathered Serpent."

"An excellent point, Miss Bristol. I shall take the utmost care not to absently wander into first-class territory."

Miss Bristol pointed out a sign on the ship's bulkhead. "That is the direction to the second-class cabins, toward the stern of the ship."

They made their way along the deck promenade, finding their way down to the second-class deck, and with the assistance of a helpful porter, located their two cabins. Professor Wexley and Professor Hollingsworth would be sharing a cabin, Miss Bristol having her own private cabin.

Professor Wexley held up a pamphlet displaying a diagram of the ship, saying, "Look here, there is a second-class dining saloon, a lounge, and an outdoor promenade solely for second-class passengers. Sadly, I fear we shall not be dining on steak and lobster this evening."

Professor Hollingsworth shrugged. "I have never found lobster to be the least bit appealing, as it bears far too much resemblance to a large ungainly insect."

George grimaced. "Now you have done it, sir; I shall never be able to eat lobster again."

After they had checked into their rooms, they returned to the second-class promenade, gazing down at the swarms of people on the docks, many of them waving their scarfs and hats, calling out their goodbyes. Miss Bristol gave a start when the raucous blast of the steam whistle sounded, announcing the ship's imminent departure.

There was a second blast fifteen minutes later, the four-hundred-foot, two-stacked steamship easing slowly away from the dock, three powerful tugboats churning up the water behind them as they guided the massive ship out of the harbor, Arthur pointing back to the Statue of Liberty and Ellis Island.

The *SS Merida's* great propellers began to turn, smoke billowing up from the stacks, the ship heading out to sea. Miss Bristol watched as Pier 14 grew smaller and smaller, her trepidation growing when she realized they would soon be sailing over a vast and unforgiving sea with no land in sight.

When they were well under way, Miss Bristol returned to her cabin, eyeing the narrow metal-framed cot and a small corner washstand with a porcelain basin and water pitcher. She took a seat on the bed, gauging the softness of the horsehair mattress. It was no match for her comfortable featherbed at home, but it would suffice. Second-class accommodations were somewhat more spartan than she had anticipated, but it was only for seven or eight days. Besides, she would be spending most of her time out on the promenade or in the lounge. There was a mirror above the washstand, a narrow wardrobe to hang her clothes, and a small chest of drawers for her personal items.

She was especially pleased to see her cabin had a porthole which could be opened, allowing fresh air to come in, the cabin proving to be somewhat stifling otherwise, especially in tropical climates. She laughed to herself, imagining how pleased Dr. Boas would be if he could see her austere quarters.

Chapter 12

That evening, Miss Bristol joined Professor Hollingsworth and Professor Wexley in the second-class dining saloon, the three of them perusing their dinner menus, a smartly dressed waiter standing at the table, pencil and pad in hand.

Professor Hollingsworth said, “What appeals to you, Miss Bristol?”

“The roast beef sounds quite good.” She looked up at the waiter, saying, “I should like the roast beef with gravy, mashed potatoes, steamed vegetables, and custard for dessert.”

The waiter nodded. “Very good, madam.”

Professor Hollingsworth said, “That does look good. I shall also have the roast beef with gravy, mashed potatoes, a side order of pickles, and rice pudding for desert. And a bottle of champagne on ice, if you would, sir. This is a rather momentous occasion.”

“Very good, sir.”

Professor Wexley said, “I shall have the baked

ham, buttered peas, mashed potatoes, with stewed apples for dessert, but no champagne. One bottle should suffice, especially as it is being paid for by Professor Hollingsworth."

Miss Bristol laughed.

When dinner had been served, Professor Hollingsworth said, "Before we begin this sumptuous feast, I should like to put forth a rather unorthodox proposal."

Professor Wexley said, "You have piqued my curiosity, sir. Feel quite free to voice your proposal."

"Since this is a scholarly archaeological expedition and we shall be in rather close company for the next three months, I would propose a temporary cessation of certain well-established social formalities. I would suggest to both of you that we address each other by our first names. That being said, you may both call me Arthur."

Miss Bristol raised her eyebrows. "Are you certain that is appropriate, sir?"

Professor Wexley laughed. "Perhaps it is the champagne talking, but I agree. For the duration of the trip, you may both call me George."

"Miss Bristol, what shall we call you?"

Miss Bristol thought for a moment, then said, "You may call me Miss Bristol. Any other name would prove far too disconcerting."

Arthur laughed. "So it shall be, Miss Bristol. And now, as is customary on a seagoing voyage such as this, I should like to propose a champagne toast."

They raised their glasses. "To what shall we be toasting, sir?"

"Let us toast to the good health of Miss Bristol, George, and Arthur—fellow voyagers aboard the *SS Merida.* Let us also toast to the success of our expedition in Teotihuacan. May our discoveries change the world as we know it, making it a better place."

"Here, here." They clinked their glasses together.

Miss Bristol added, "Let us not change the world too much, Arthur, as I have grown quite fond of this one." Miss Bristol found it mildly unsettling to be calling Professor Hollingsworth by his first name, but she also quite liked it.

That night Miss Bristol had a rather difficult time falling asleep, listening to the low rumblings of the ship's massive steam engines as it plowed through the rolling seas, the ship rocking at times far more than Miss Bristol had anticipated. Eventually sleep overtook her, the rocking motion of the ship proving in the end to be quite soothing.

On the second day of their journey, as they sat in the lounge enjoying a light lunch, Miss Bristol noticed George studying a bearded man seated alone at a nearby table.

Arthur also noticed George's rapt attention to the bearded man. "Why do you keep looking at that man? Do you know him?"

"It is very possible that I do, in a manner of speaking. Wait here, I shall return shortly."

He dashed off to his cabin, returning five minutes later with a book, opening it to a photograph of a bearded man. He gave a victorious laugh. "I knew it, I knew it was him."

"Who is that man?"

George held up the book, Miss Bristol reading the title out loud. "*Edison's Conquest of Mars*. What manner of book is that? Surely he is not referring to the great Thomas Edison?"

"It is a marvelous and fantastical novel by Garret P. Serviss, the very man we are currently looking at. He is indeed referring to the great inventor, Thomas Edison."

Miss Bristol studied the photo, then the man seated at the table. "It does quite resemble him."

"I shall go over and invite him to join us for lunch."

"Is that appropriate? He doesn't know you from Adam."

"He is sitting alone, it would be a friendly gesture.

He can always decline if he wishes, as is his right."

"What is his novel about? How does it concern Thomas Edison?"

"It is a fantastical tale of a war between Earth and the inhabitants of Mars. In the novel, Thomas Edison and a number of other well-known scientists travel to the red planet and use their wits to defeat the warlike Martians. They are highly advanced beings with sophisticated technology and intent on our destruction. They also possess superior intellect and powerful machines, such as heat rays and anti-gravity devices. It is a continuation of *War of the Worlds*, the popular novel by H.G. Wells."

Miss Bristol looked more than dubious. "A novel about warlike Martians and Thomas Edison? To be honest, it sounds quite preposterous."

George continued, "The story is fantastical, of course, but there are deeper truths to be found within his fictional stories, as they are filled with many well established scientific facts. He is a highly educated man, the book stating that he received a degree in science from Cornell University, and a law degree from our own Columbia University. He has been a journalist at the New York Sun, and Andrew Carnegie himself invited him to lecture across the country on any number of scientific matters. Carnegie with impressed with his ability to relate complex scientific principles and theories in terms easily understood by those with little or no scientific background."

Miss Bristol said, "He does sound like a rather interesting man. You have my blessing; let us see if he shall dine with us."

To George's great delight, Mr. Serviss did agree to join them, and was soon seated at their table.

"This is lovely, and I do thank you for your kind invitation to dine with you. Professor Wexley, it sounds as if you are quite familiar with my books, which of course pleases me no end. You are all from Columbia University?"

Arthur nodded. "I am a professor of anthropology, George is a noted physics professor, and Miss Bristol is a brilliant and invaluable research assistant."

"How marvelous to see a young woman entering the scientific arena. I have the utmost admiration for you, Miss Bristol, truly I do. I wish only the best for you. I always say, 'a brilliant mind is a brilliant mind, and that is all we need to know.'"

"You are too kind, sir."

George said, "May I ask you a question, sir, one related to your writings?"

"Of course you may."

"In your estimation, is it possible that intelligent

beings from distant worlds have already visited this little planet of ours?"

Mr. Serviss smiled. "A question I have been asked more than a few times, I assure you, and my answer is always the same. Our world is many hundreds of millions, possibly billions of years old. Human scientific advancements really only began a few thousand years ago, but here we are today with electric lights, aeroplanes, buildings that touch the sky, marvelous new life-saving medical procedures, the ability to communicate with each other across vast distances using the telegraph, and now to speak to each other using Alexander Graham Bell's telephone. Having said that, can you imagine what our scientific advancements shall look like in ten thousand years, or a hundred thousand years, or even a million years? Surely we shall be traveling to distant worlds in ships such as those described by H.G. Wells. Now, imagine if you would, other worlds, worlds where their scientific advancements began five million years ago. It truly boggles the mind. So, my answer is yes, it is entirely possible that our world has been visited by beings from a distant planet, although it may have been many thousands of years in the past, back when we were still running around whacking each other on the head with wooden clubs."

Miss Bristol burst out laughing. “You paint a most engaging picture, sir.”

Arthur said, “And you make a very convincing argument. I can tell you with unabashed certainty that the three of us also believe the world has been visited by beings from another world.”

Mr. Serviss raised his glass. “To science and to common sense; may they live on forever.”

George asked, “May I inquire as to your final destination, sir?”

“It is Havana, for a much needed respite from writing and lecturing. The weather there is marvelous, and I have a number of dear old friends who live there. Is Havana also your final destination, sir?”

“We are on an archeological expedition to Teotihuacan, to study The Temple of the Feathered Serpent, along with the Pyramids of the Sun and Moon.”

“The Temple of the Feathered Serpent, what a marvelous name it is! It all sounds quite thrilling, perhaps I shall write a fantastical novel about just such an adventure as yours.” He gave a jovial laugh.

When dinner was done, George asked Mr. Serviss if he would sign his copy of *Edison's Conquest of Mars*, Mr. Serviss readily agreeing to do so. Arthur brought out his folding Kodak, taking a photograph of George and Mr. Serviss, George proudly holding up the signed volume.

Miss Bristol spent the fourth day of their voyage sequestered in her cabin, quite ill from the swaying and rocking motion of the ship as they made their way through turbulent seas amidst a rather violent storm, rain spattering wildly against her cabin porthole, the roar of the wind interrupted by brilliant sporadic flashes of lightning and deafening claps of thunder.

She emerged the following morning to brilliant sunshine and blue skies, finding Arthur and George standing out on the promenade, pointing to a dark line running along the horizon.

Arthur smiled when he saw her. "Miss Bristol, I do hope you have quite recovered from the dreadful storm?"

"Thank you for asking, Arthur. I am quite well, now that the stormy seas have calmed."

George pointed to the horizon. "Cuba is well in sight. It won't be long until we are strolling along beneath swaying coconut palm trees, listening to the waves breaking on the warm sandy beaches. I must not forget to bring back several boxes of Cuban cigars for my father. He specifically requested them, claiming they are the best in the world."

Miss Bristol said, "I have never understood what would possess a person to do such a thing as smoke a cigar. The smell is quite ghastly, like burnt rags and old boots."

George laughed. "I shall not mention to my father your opinion of his cigars, but in strict confidence, I quite agree with you."

Arthur said, "We are getting closer to the port, I can just make out some of your swaying coconut palm trees."

Miss Bristol eyed the Havana coastline. "Havana does sound lovely, but I am quite looking forward to the train ride from Veracruz to Mexico City. I have read that the scenery along the way is stunningly beautiful and exceedingly diverse, quite unique."

The *SS Merida* arrived in Havana an hour later, anchoring in Havana Bay, one of the busiest ports in the Caribbean. Miss Bristol gazed at the sea of masts and smokestacks, cargo lighters, and wooden boats ferrying passengers and cargo to and from the shore.

After some discussion, the three travelers decided to go ashore for the day, Miss Bristol having carefully read a bulletin posted in the second-class lounge stating that they must first contact the purser for a landing pass, and be well-prepared to show their passports to the customs officials. Miss Bristol laughingly advised Arthur not to mention his infectious laugh or they might be spending the rest of their trip in quarantine.

With landing passes in hand, they boarded a wooden launch boat, the pilot announcing that the last boat back to the *SS Merida* left the docks at five o'clock sharp. If they missed that, they would be forced to spend the next nine days in Havana.

Miss Bristol laughed, "I can only imagine the look on Dr. Boas' face if he received a telegram saying we would be spending nine days in Havana."

Arthur nodded his agreement. "I fear that would bring a rather sudden and ignominious end to my professorship at Columbia."

Miss Bristol found Havana to be quite intoxicating, falling in love with the sights and sounds of the port city, with its quaint cobblestone streets, Spanish Baroque churches, and lush leafy plazas. They stopped at a vendor selling hot roasted peanuts, served to them in small paper cones. Miss Bristol tried a drink called Guarapo, freshly pressed sugarcane juice served on ice, finding it to be sweet and cold, providing welcome relief from the hot Havana sun. Arthur grinned when he spotted a vendor selling Jugo de Piña, or fresh pineapple juice, strained and poured over ice.

Miss Bristol experienced a mortifying moment when a smiling vendor selling flowers asked Arthur if he would like to buy a bouquet for his beautiful young wife.

Arthur graciously replied, "Miss Bristol is a university associate sir, not my wife, and a respected anthropological research assistant at Columbia University."

The vendor grinned. "Of course, sir, as you say, your research assistant." He laughed, giving Arthur a dreadfully salacious wink as he walked away.

Arthur turned to Miss Bristol, saying, "I apologize for his error, and for his repugnant behavior. It was uncalled for, and most inappropriate."

Miss Bristol had managed to gather her wits about her, replying, "Thank you, Arthur. I do appreciate your understanding and your kind comments."

"Of course, Miss Bristol."

Miss Bristol was well aware that to even make jest of the embarrassing incident would be most inappropriate. It should simply be forgotten—a task which ultimately proved rather difficult for her to accomplish.

George returned half an hour later, a bottle of rum in one hand and three boxes of Cuban cigars in the other. "This should please my father no end, a bottle of aged rum and three boxes of fine Cuban cigars." He laughed. "The vendor told me in strictest confidence that Cuban cigars are made from burnt rags and old boots."

Miss Bristol laughed. “How dreadful!”

They stopped for a short time to listen to a festive gathering of street musicians playing guitars, conga drums, and bongos, the singers keeping the rhythm with maracas, many of the spectators dancing to the lively music.

The hours flew by, Miss Bristol buying a number of colorful souvenirs for herself and her parents, including two silver souvenir spoons for her mother’s collection. After a late lunch of empanadas, tostones, and Cuban style tamales, the three travelers headed back to the docks, Miss Bristol adamant that they not miss the final boat back to the *SS Merida.*

Chapter 13

Four days later the three adventurers watched as the port city of Veracruz drew closer to them, George saying, "It is a much larger port than I had thought it to be, although it is no rival for the Port of New York."

Miss Bristol eyed the rows of warehouses lining the docks, dozens upon dozens of ships loading and unloading their cargos, a curious mixture of sailing ships and modern steamships. She said, "Veracruz is an important center of commerce, Mexico exporting any number of goods such as coffee, sugar, tobacco, and vanilla to Europe and to the Americas."

George said, "How do you come to know such things, Miss Bristol?"

"I read numerous pamphlets about both Havana and Veracruz while making our travel arrangements. I find it to be quite fascinating. It is equally as interesting to study modern civilizations as it is to study ancient ones. After all, there was a time when the ancient civilizations we study were the modern ones."

Arthur said, “Well said, and quite true. I admire your sense of curiosity—that is what makes a good scientist.”

“I have always found such things to be interesting, even as a young girl, much to my mother’s dismay. She would have preferred me to take a far greater interest in dolls and ribbons and pretty dresses, but such things held little appeal to me. I was far more interested in knowing what makes the sky blue, how birds know when to fly south, why ice floats, why there are so many languages, if there are colors we have never seen—things of that nature.”

Arthur laughed, “And how did your parents respond to such profound questions as those?”

“My mother thought it to be most unusual, that I was an odd child, but my father was more than happy to answer all my questions as best he could, going so far as to buy me a set of encyclopedias he found in a used book shop when I was ten years old. My mother still has grave doubts about my studies in anthropology, warning me that I shall never marry, believing that men can’t abide highly educated women.”

“I have great admiration for your father, and I would say to your mother that the world is changing, it is not the same world as the one she grew up in. I can tell you that my parents owned a bakery, insisting that I join the family business after I had finished high school. Despite their wishes, I chose to continue my education, choosing anthropology over baking bread. It took several years for them to accept my decision, but as time passed they made their peace with it, proudly telling their friends that their son was a professor at Columbia University. So you see, you are not alone in the dilemma you faced as a young girl. The best advice I can give is to spend as much of your life as you can doing what you love. It is your life to do with as you see fit. Did you grow up in Brooklyn?"

"I did. My parents still have their home there, a lovely old row house. I am quite fond of the home, as it holds many cherished memories for me. The encyclopedias my father gave me still sit on a shelf in my bedroom."

George said, "I live in Brooklyn with my parents, in a stately old home with a large gated yard. It has been in our family for several generations, but one day I shall have a grand home of my own, marry and raise a family."

Their conversation was interrupted by the blast of a steam whistle as the *SS Merida* approached the dock at Veracruz, guided by two large tugboats, their stacks belching out clouds of black smoke.

"We shall be disembarking soon; let us gather up

our belongings."

Miss Bristol said, "I have arranged for the porters to carry our steamer trunks to the hotel. We shall spend one night here, and the following morning board the train which takes us to Mexico City."

Several hours later, amidst the noise and bustle of the vibrant port city, they made their way down the gangplank, setting foot once again on solid ground.

Arthur gazed at the port, saying, "It is like stepping back in time. These cobblestone streets are from days gone by, as is the architecture, with its distinct Spanish influence."

"In some ways it is quite similar to Havana. Have you ever seen such a wide variety of people? It is a wondrous sight to behold. It inspires me to travel the world and visit a hundred different cities."

Arthur laughed. "Perhaps one day, but I suggest we first locate our hotel. I shall hail a carriage. What is the name of the hotel where we shall be staying?"

Miss Bristol pulled a folded pamphlet from her handbag. "I have reserved rooms for us at the Gran Hotel Diligencias. It is close to the port, and renowned for its elegant accommodations, being called by some the finest hotel in Veracruz."

"Good heavens, what will Dr. Boas have to say about that?"

Miss Bristol said, "Dr. Boas mentioned nothing of our hotel accommodations, only those aboard the steamship and the railway lines."

George burst out laughing. "Well done, Miss Bristol."

"I do hope you both brought formal attire suitable for such an elegant hotel. I doubt we should be allowed entry into the dining room while wearing khaki expedition wear and pith helmets."

Arthur said, "Of course, Miss Bristol. I shall be smartly dressed in black tie and top hat."

"And I shall be wearing a lovely evening gown, purchased just for the occasion."

George said, "Black tie and top hat for me also. They shall never suspect we are but rough and tumble adventurers on our way to a dig in Teotihuacan."

Dinner that evening proved to be quite an adventure in dining for the three of them, consisting of a seven-course meal with three kinds of wine, and trays of delightful pastries and sweets for dessert.

As they were standing up to leave, Arthur pulled a folding Kodak from his coat pocket. "We must record this historical moment for posterity."

He handed the camera to a waiter, the three of them posing for a photograph in their elegant attire. Miss Bristol said, "We must each get a print of this photograph."

Arthur nodded, saying, "I agree, but we must take great care to see that Dr. Boas does not receive a print, presenting him only with images of us in our expedition wear, shovels in hand, sweat on our brow."

Miss Bristol laughed.

The following morning found the three companions riding through the city of Veracruz in a horse-drawn carriage, making their way to Veracruz Station. Miss Bristol studied the building's gently arched façade and classical columns as they approached the station. "It is magnificent, rivaling the train stations of New York."

Miss Bristol stepped down from the carriage, George and Arthur right behind her. Porters appeared, loading their steamer trunks onto a large cart, wheeling them away to be loaded onto the train. The interior of the station was crowded and noisy, wide wooden benches lining the tiled floor, overhead ceiling fans turning slowly in the warm humid air. The walls were decorated with numerous faded travel posters and a large painted timetable board, uniformed porters calling out names and destinations as they walked through the teeming throng of travelers.

As they were maneuvering their way through the crowd, George said, "Shall we buy something to eat for the train ride? It is at minimum a twelve hour journey, probably more."

Miss Bristol said, "If you wish, but I was told by the rail line agent that there would be a second-class dining car available to us."

Arthur stepped over to a nearby fruit vendor, eyeing his cart of wares. He smiled at the man, saying, "I see you have fresh pineapple slices, bananas, and oranges, but there is one I don't recognize. What is this brown fruit called, the one resembling small apples?"

The vendor held one up, saying, "Chicozapote, very good, sweet."

Arthur returned with a woven basket filled with a variety of fresh fruits, George raising his eyebrows. "You have enough fruit there to feed a small army."

Miss Bristol eyed the heavily laden basket. "Is that fresh pineapple?"

"It is supposed to be quite refreshing during the heat of the day."

"It is quite warm and humid here, but not surprising for a tropical lowland. Despite the heat, it is a fascinating city; there are new sights to see at every turn, and so much to learn."

They made their way through the station and out to the train platforms, the enormous vaulted iron canopies providing protection from the blazing sun. Arthur eyed the massive black steam locomotive, hissing and belching smoke as it prepared for the long journey to Mexico City, a dozen train cars lined up behind it.

Miss Bristol approached one of the porters, showing her ticket to him. He pointed to the fifth train car, saying, "Go, go. Second-class."

Miss Bristol asked, "Where is the second-class dining car?" She pointed to the train cars with a questioning look.

"First-class only, no second-class."

They boarded the fifth train car, a uniformed ticket inspector punching their tickets, motioning for them to sit on the long wooden benches that ran the length of the car. George took a seat on the bench, frowning. "There is very little padding on the benches, considering it is a twelve hour trip. To be quite honest, I was expecting comfortably padded seats."

Miss Bristol nodded her head in agreement. "I can see that a number of passengers have brought pillows with them."

"An excellent thought; I shall fold up my jacket and use it as a cushion."

Arthur said, "Did you notice if there was a second-class dining car?"

"There is not—I was given inaccurate information by the rail line office, the porter telling me just now that the only dining car is for first-class passengers."

"Perhaps we should send a telegraph to Dr. Boas, asking his permission to purchase first-class tickets so that we may enjoy a pleasant lunch."

Miss Bristol laughed. "That would please him no end, I am sure of it."

George shrugged. "At least we have plenty of fruit."

Finally they heard the blast of the train's steam whistle, the conductor leaning out of the car, crying out, "Última llamada, última llamada!"

George said, "What is he saying?"

The man seated next to him answered, "Last call, last call."

"Thank you, sir."

The man added, "I overheard your discussion regarding the second-class dining car. You will be pleased to know we shall be making stops at Orizaba and Córdoba, where you may purchase meals from station vendors."

"That is most welcome news."

The steam whistle sounded again, the train cars squealing and lurching forward, slowly gathering speed. Miss Bristol peered out of the open window as the train rolled through Veracruz, heading toward the lush forests and jungles in the distance.

George said, “Look at the orchards, they are grand, although I am uncertain what kind of fruit they bear. Perhaps they are mango trees?”

Arthur pointed ahead of them, saying, “Look there, I believe that is an orange grove. How lucky they are to have an unending supply of fresh oranges.”

An hour later the train was rumbling and rattling through dense tropical forests and jungles, Miss Bristol pointing to a group of strange looking trees with enormous winding roots rising well above the ground. “Good heavens, look at those odd trees. I’ve never seen anything like them before. Their roots are enormous.”

The man sitting next to George said, “They are called ceiba trees, quite unusual looking. The other trees you see growing next to the tracks are mahogany and ebony trees.”

“There are so many of them, it’s quite astounding.”

George called out, “I just saw two brightly colored parrots! Imagine that, parrots flying freely about, like the pigeons of New York.”

Miss Bristol cried out, “A monkey! I saw a wild monkey frolicking in the trees next to the river. I have never seen such a sight as this. This jungle appears to have no end.”

After several more hours, the train slowed slightly

as it headed up a steep winding incline, Miss Bristol pointing to the forested slopes of the mountains ahead of them. She pulled a map from her handbag, studying it. "The mountains are called the Sierra Madre Oriental. They form a plateau, the Valley of Mexico. That is where we shall find Mexico City."

She glanced at Arthur, seated next to her, his head nodding, eyes closed, Miss Bristol wondering how anyone could sleep amidst such glorious scenery. This was absolutely thrilling. She held her breath as the train crossed over a massive ravine hundreds of feet deep, the train rumbling across a narrow wood and steel trestle bridge.

George was engrossed in a book, pausing now and then to scribble notes onto a small notepad.

"Whatever are you doing? You are missing the most magnificent scenic views."

"I am attempting to make sense of Albert Einstein's 1905 Special Theory of Relativity. His paper is titled, *On the Electrodynamics of Moving Bodies*."

"Would that include moving bodies such as the train you are riding on?" Miss Bristol laughed.

"In fact it would, Miss Bristol. The motion of objects is relative. To us, seated on the train, the train seems to be standing still, everyone on the train remaining in the same relative position, the interior of the train unchanging. But to someone in the jungle watching the train pass, we are all racing by at twenty-five or thirty miles an hour. The question is, are we sitting still, or are we moving? It is all relative, depending on the position of the observer."

Miss Bristol said, "That seems quite obvious."

"There is far more to Einstein's theory than that, I assure you—especially if the train happens to be traveling at the speed of light, one hundred and eighty-six thousand miles per second."

"It would be a very short trip indeed at such a speed, and we should have no time at all to admire the lovely scenery."

"And perhaps when we arrived in Mexico City, time and space would have ceased to exist for us. It is all quite a mystery. Einstein is absolutely brilliant, but his theories can be quite unfathomable."

The train finally reached the plateau, the tropical jungles far behind them, rolling hills and golden grasses stretching into the distance ahead of them.

"Look there, a cactus, the first I have ever seen. They are quite unusual looking with those long spikes."

George said, "I should not like to use one for a cushion."

Miss Bristol laughed. "What a frightening

thought."

Arthur was awake now, gazing out the window at an approaching village, studying several dozen white-washed adobe huts surrounded by small orchards.

Miss Bristol was looking at her map. "It is said there was an enormous lake in this area at one time, but it was drained to allow for the expansion of the city."

Arthur said, "Yes, Lake Texoco. Tenochtitlan was the capital of the Aztec Empire, built on an island in the middle of Lake Texcoco, becoming a large and sophisticated city, with temples, canals, marketplaces, and palaces. It must have been a marvelous site during the reign of the Aztecs, with its magnificent floating gardens. It was a bustling metropolis even back then, with a population of over three hundred thousand people. After the Spanish conquest in 1521, Tenochtitlan was largely destroyed, and Mexico City was built atop its ruins."

George said, "You are quite familiar with this area?"

"I have studied a great deal about the Aztecs and Mayans and Teotihuacan, but this is my first visit to the area."

George said, "I find it to be quite confusing. Was it the Aztecs or the Mayans who built Teotihuacan?"

“It was neither of them. The Aztecs lived in central Mexico, the Mayans living much earlier and farther to the south. When the Aztecs discovered Teotihuacan, it had been abandoned for at least several hundred years. It was built by a Mesoamerican civilization around 100 AD, but very little is known about them. It was the Aztecs who named it Teotihuacan, which means ‘the place where gods were created.’”

Chapter 14

At long last the train rolled into Mexico City, Miss Bristol startled by the immensity of the city and the majestic neoclassical architecture of the buildings. "How astonishing, it bears some great resemblance to New York City. Look at the grand scale of the buildings."

Arthur's eyes were not on the buildings, however, they were on a formation of armed soldiers marching down a broad avenue.

"As interesting as the city is, we must not linger here, continuing on to Teotihuacan as quickly as we are able. There have been stories recently in the newspapers about a possible revolution brewing in Mexico. They say there is great discontent with the oppressive rule of Porfirio Díaz, that the vast majority of the population lives in poverty, while a small elite group holds the wealth and power. There have been a number of skirmishes between rebels and the soldiers in rural areas, but nothing in Mexico City as yet."

"Are we in any danger?"

"The sight of soldiers is a little concerning, but we shall be leaving the city bright and early in the morning."

They rose at sunrise, after spending the night in a small but comfortable hotel, a horse-drawn carriage arriving soon after they had finished breakfast.

George said, "That is a curious carriage, it must hold at least a dozen or more passengers. It almost looks like a miniature train car."

Miss Bristol said, "It is called an omnibus, large enough to carry our steamer trunks and quite a number of passengers. All our other supplies should already be there, our canvas tents in place. If the foreman has done as I requested, the ten laborers shall be arriving tomorrow."

Arthur said, "Well done, Miss Bristol. You have thought of everything."

They boarded the omnibus, along with six other passengers who spoke no English, the porters loading their steamer trunks onto the roof of the carriage, strapping them down securely.

"Arre, arre!" The driver called out to the team of four sturdy horses as he released the brake lever, gripping the reins as the carriage rolled forward.

Arthur gazed out the window as they passed

through a poverty stricken section of Mexico City, large decrepit buildings now packed with dozens of families living in dismal conditions. The narrow, dusty crowded streets were filled with the raucous sounds of street vendors hawking their wares—food, old clothing, and used housewares—children playing, and the lively music of street musicians. The smells of smoke, cooking, refuse, and decaying waste hung heavily in the air.

Arthur said, "This is why there is growing unrest in Mexico, why people are unhappy with the oppressive rule of Porfirio Díaz, and why there may soon be a revolution."

Miss Bristol was silent, her eyes on the overcrowded streets, on the faces of people living in such distressing poverty.

When the city was behind them, Miss Bristol found herself absently admiring the green and silver hues of the low shrubs and wild sage that dotted the arid terrain. The journey proved to be uneventful, something which pleased Miss Bristol. The omnibus carried them past a number of small villages along the way, their church bell towers rising above low whitewashed buildings. They stopped several times to let the other passengers off, eventually leaving Miss Bristol, Arthur, and George as the sole remaining passengers aboard the carriage.

George pulled out his gold pocket watch, tapping it. "It will be at least another hour until we arrive. I shall be glad when we are there. It has been a marvelous trip, but has proven to be quite tiring. I am more than ready to sit in a soft chair that does not shake or rock or bounce."

Miss Bristol laughed. "As am I." She pointed out the window, saying, "Look over there, that long building with the row of arches. It is in a state of great disrepair, the gardens overgrown, as if it has been long abandoned."

Arthur nodded. "It is a hacienda, no doubt once inhabited by wealthy landowners. It must have been a ranch or a farm. Time marches on, bringing change with it, even for stately homes such as that."

The landscape gradually became rockier, rugged, Arthur giving a sudden shout. "Look there! In the distance, it is the Pyramid of the Sun, the tallest structure at Teotihuacan."

Miss Bristol gazed in wonder at the massive pyramid bathed in the warm afternoon sun. "It is breathtaking. I can scarcely believe it, but we are almost there, we are almost in Teotihuacan."

The carriage rolled on, the Pyramid of the Moon coming into view. They finally slowed to a halt on the

Avenue of the Dead, Miss Bristol listening to the eerie silence that surrounded them, her eyes on the time-worn ruins of a once-vast and formidable empire.

Arthur stepped down from the carriage, looking around him, spotting three white canvas tents in the distance, calling out to the driver, pointing to the tents. He climbed back into the carriage, the driver releasing the brake and flicking the reins, turning the heavy omnibus toward the expedition campsite.

The omnibus rolled to a halt in front of the three large rectangular tents, the driver setting the brake lever, climbing down and opening the carriage door. Miss Bristol, Arthur, and George stepped down onto the uneven, overgrown surface of the Avenue of the Dead, the ancient roadway bordered by remnants of collapsed stone buildings and mounds of previously excavated rubble.

Arthur turned toward the Pyramid of the Sun, studying it. "It must have been a stunning sight, the Avenue of the Dead paved with slabs of white limestone, the pyramids gleaming in the sun, their smooth surfaces brightly painted in red and white."

Miss Bristol said, "I wish I could have seen it."

"It was only a few years ago that Leopoldo Batres was here, attempting to reconstruct the Pyramid of the Moon. Perhaps one day the pyramids shall look as they did two thousand years ago."

The driver offloaded their steamer trunks, moving them to the appropriate tents. When he was done, Arthur gave him a substantial tip for his services, the man thanking him profusely in Spanish.

Miss Bristol spotted a rather disheveled looking man heading toward them, dressed in worn canvas trousers, scuffed leather boots, a stained khaki shirt with rolled up sleeves, a misshapen wide-brimmed felt hat in one hand. Despite his appearance, he had a wide smile on his face, waving to them.

"Hello, hello, to you all."

Miss Bristol greeted him kindly. "You are Ezra Crowder, the foreman we engaged to oversee the dig?"

"Yes, madam, I am he, Ezra Crowder, at your disposal."

Arthur stepped over and shook Ezra's hand. "It is a pleasure to meet you, sir. I am Professor Hollingsworth, this is Professor Wexley, and, as you know, this young lady is Miss Bristol, our invaluable research assistant at Columbia University. You have done marvelously, the tents and supplies all looking to be in order. The laborers will be arriving tomorrow?"

"Yes, tomorrow, the laborers will be arriving then,

along with a cook to prepare the meals."

Miss Bristol smiled to herself. Arthur seemed to go out of his way to tell people that she was a research assistant at Columbia.

She studied the foreman, an odd feeling coming over her. She prided herself on thinking the best of people, trusting them until she learned they could not be trusted, to accept them as they were, no matter their lot in life. As they say, "There but for the grace of God, go I." Despite all this, there was something unsettling about him, something vaguely untrustworthy, a feeling that did not diminish with time. Perhaps it was a necessity for his survival here, living a hard scrabble life in Mexico City, eking out an uncertain living as a hired foreman.

Ezra gave Miss Bristol an ingratiating smile. "It is a great pleasure to meet you, Miss Bristol. You might be interested to know that I have walked past your great Columbia University on more than one occasion."

"Good heavens, you are from New York?"

"I was originally from that area, but moved to Mexico City twelve years ago. It seemed to be a land filled with opportunity, and to be quite honest, my life in New York had become complicated."

"I see. It is nice to meet a fellow New Yorker. As

Professor Hollingsworth has already mentioned, you have done a marvelous job setting up our camp."

"Thank you, Miss Bristol." He tipped his well-worn hat to her.

George said, "Perhaps we should unpack our trunks and get settled in, change into our expedition wear. I should not like to be wearing this suit as I crawl through an ancient tunnel."

Miss Bristol laughed. "I should agree with you, sir. We must change into more appropriate clothing."

Ezra said, "The cook does not arrive until tomorrow, so I shall be preparing your dinner this evening."

George laughed, "Wonderful, thank you, Ezra. I am far less than proficient in the culinary arts."

"Of course."

Miss Bristol headed to her tent, opening her trunk and removing her expedition wear: a long khaki skirt with wide pockets; a long-sleeved button-up shirt to protect her from the noonday sun; sturdy lace-up leather boots, protection from snakes and scorpions; a colorful neckerchief and pith helmet, added protection from the blazing sun.

She donned the clothing, placing a field notebook and pencil in her skirt pocket, along with a pocket knife, brass compass, and a pair of cotton gloves. Standing in front of a small mirror, she studied her reflection, a smile crossing her face. She looked like an archeologist. She must ask Arthur to take photographs of them during the dig— photographs she could show to her parents. Her mother had not yet fully accepted her choice of occupations, often telling her it would be best if Miss Bristol were to meet a nice man, settle down and raise a family. Miss Bristol gave a resigned sigh. It was a new world, one her mother was not familiar with, but perhaps there was a chance a photograph of her proudly standing in front of The Temple of the Feathered Serpent might change her mind.

Miss Bristol emerged from her tent to see Arthur and George dressed in their expedition garb, noting the heavy Webley revolver holstered at Arthur's side.

"What on earth is that revolver for?"

Arthur shrugged. "It is for snakes—there many different varieties of them to be found in remote places such as this, some of them with two legs."

"Are you speaking of bandits?"

"It is always best to be prepared."

"I suppose you are right; one never knows."

George pointed to the towering Pyramid of the Sun. "Shall we stroll down that way to get a closer look? It is magnificent, truly a monumental sight to behold."

Arthur pulled out his folding pocket camera, taking a photograph of the pyramid. “Shall we go?”

They headed down the Avenue of the Dead, Miss Bristol saying, “This roadway is far longer than I had imagined it to be. You say it was once paved with white limestone?”

Arthur nodded. “Quite correct, white limestone covered with smooth lime stucco, which was then brightly painted in certain areas, often times a bright red. It is overgrown now, covered with rubble, weeds, grass, and spiny shrubs, a far cry from what it once was. The Avenue of the Dead is over two miles long, running directly through Teotihuacan, connecting the Pyramid of the Sun, Pyramid of the Moon, and the Ciudadela—the area which, among other structures, holds the Temple of the Feathered Serpent. At the peak of the Aztecs’ power, over a hundred thousand people lived here.”

George turned around, glancing back at the camp. “May I ask what your initial impressions are of Ezra, our illustrious foreman?”

Arthur pursed his lips. “I do not wish to speak ill of others, but to be quite honest, I would have to say I have my doubts regarding his trustworthiness, although he did a marvelous job setting up camp. Miss Bristol, what are your thoughts on our Mr. Crowder?”

"I would agree with your evaluation. He presents a most ingratiating demeanor, but I sense he is hiding a darker side. I can only speculate on what he was referring to when he said his life in New York had become complicated."

George shrugged, "Maybe the police were after him, or maybe he owed a large sum of money to the Five Points Gang. There are a thousand reasons why he may have left, but as long as he performs his duties, I suggest we let sleeping dogs lie. Perhaps such behavior is a necessity for survival in a rugged land such as this."

Arthur said, "I suppose it would be challenging, living day-to-day in conditions such as these."

Miss Bristol added, "On the other hand, I would believe there are many thousands of people living in Mexico City who are as honest as the day is long."

Arthur nodded his agreement. "That is also true. I propose we trust Ezra, but be on guard, be vigilant. Above all, we should make no mention to him of our true purpose here, of the secret tunnel where Beaumont discovered the fabric sleeve."

Miss Bristol said, "We have the map drawn by Frederick Beaumont noting the precise location of the hidden tunnel, but it might be best not to go there directly, visiting our other dig sites first, searching for what artifacts we might find. I expect we shall need a minimum of three large crates of artifacts to appease Dr. Boas upon our return."

"An excellent plan. We shall pretend to accidentally stumble upon the hidden tunnel, exploring it by ourselves, mentioning nothing to Ezra Crowder if we do find any curious objects left by a certain group of mysterious visitors."

Miss Bristol laughed. "Perhaps we shall discover a ship from a distant world, one such as those described by your new writer friend, Garrett P. Serviss."

Arthur said, "A marvelous thought, Miss Bristol. We could fly it victoriously back to Columbia University in less than an hour."

"Imagine the look of surprise on Dr. Boas' face when he saw us hovering above Schermerhorn Hall, waving down to him from on high."

George laughed, "That would be a sight to see. All jesting aside, we must not forget the true origin of the fabric sleeve. There is a real possibility that we shall find similar astonishing objects in Beaumont's tunnel."

"You are quite right, this is not a fantastical adventure—we hold in our hands solid physical proof of the presence of otherworldly beings, whoever they may have been, wherever they may have come from."

They approached the Pyramid of the Sun, Miss Bristol gazing up in wonder at the monumental proportions of the stone structure, eyeing the series of wide grand stairways leading to the top of the pyramid. “The pyramids here are quite different from the pyramids of Egypt.”

Arthur said, “Unlike Egyptian pyramids, these are stepped pyramids, each tier having a broad flat terrace. They were used as platforms for religious ceremonies, not as burial tombs. The Pyramid of the Sun stands two hundred and sixteen feel tall and was built almost two thousand years ago. The top of it is flat now, but it once held a large temple. The Pyramid of the Moon stands one hundred and forty-one feet tall. A portion of it was reconstructed by Leopoldo Batres about ten years ago.”

“And the Temple of the Feathered Serpent?”

“It is sixty-six feet tall, holding carvings of Quetzalcóatl, the Feathered Serpent, and Tláloc the Rain God, among others. The carvings are stunning, simply magnificent. I can only imagine what they looked like when coated with smooth white lime stucco and brightly painted.”

Miss Bristol made her way over to the base of the Pyramid of the Sun, running a hand across its rough stone surface. “It is truly a wonder to be here in the presence of such an ancient and venerable structure. It gives me chills."

Arthur said, "There is a dark side to it, of course, as there are with most civilizations. There were a great many human sacrifices performed here, perhaps hundreds of thousands, some long before the appearance of the Aztecs. It was believed by a number of Mesoamerican cultures that only a great and continuing sacrifice to the gods would sustain the Universe. Everything they did was done to appease the gods. They believed the gods had sacrificed themselves to create this world, and they were expected by the gods to do the same."

Miss Bristol nodded. "It is a sad truth that countless humans across time have lost their lives to such deadly rituals. It was all they knew then—they did not know the science of the stars and planets, of the moon, of the ever changing weather systems and the natural cycles and causes of rain and drought. The sacrifices were their attempt to control the environment around them, rain and successful harvests being crucial to their survival."

"We have come a long way since then, but in some ways we are still primitive beings."

George said, "On that very somber note, shall we head back to camp? I am quite famished and looking forward to whatever meal Ezra shall be preparing for us. Perhaps it will be steak and lobster, baked potatoes, and a fine wine."

Arthur laughed. "I would not set my hopes quite so high."

Chapter 15

Half an hour later they were back at the campsite, Ezra standing next to a blazing campfire, a large cast iron skillet resting on a metal grate above the fire.

Ezra waved to them. "I have prepared your evening meal: authentic bean and cheese enchiladas, a variety of fresh fruit, and local cheese and bread, queso fresco with bolillos."

Arthur rubbed his hands together. "It sounds wonderful. We are all quite famished from our long journey."

After dinner, Ezra scrubbed clean the dishes and returned to his tent at the workers' campsite, located a hundred yards away from the main camp. The three friends gathered in the central tent, studying the maps that Arthur had spread out before them on a wooden table.

Arthur pointed to four circles he had drawn on a map of Teotihuacan. "I have chosen these locations for our official digs. During these digs we shall most certainly uncover numerous common household artifacts such as pottery used for cooking and storage, obsidian tools, small clay figurines, and a large number of stone beads and greenstone pendants worn as jewelry."

He pointed to a barely visible red dot on the map. "This is the location of the tunnel entrance where the fabric sleeve was found. Beaumont mentioned in his notes that the tunnel had collapsed at one point and he chose to dig elsewhere, not trusting the stability of the tunnel walls and roof. He suspected it was a tunnel built by looters."

Miss Bristol frowned. "Are you certain it will be safe?"

Arthur said, "I am only certain of one thing, Miss Bristol; we must explore Beaumont's tunnel to the fullest extent we are able. Nothing is of more importance than this."

George said, "If it becomes necessary, the laborers can use wooden beams to structurally support the tunnel."

"An excellent idea, but hopefully it shall not become necessary."

George covered his mouth, stifling a yawn. "I am quite exhausted from the day's journey. I believe I shall retire for the night."

Arthur said, "As shall I. We must get a good night's sleep; the laborers are arriving early tomorrow morning. Once we have enough artifacts to satisfy Dr. Boas, we can begin our exploration of Beaumont's tunnel."

Arthur walked Miss Bristol to her tent, unholstering his revolver and handing it to her. "I should like you to have this when you are alone in your tent, Miss Bristol. Make certain you tie your tent flaps securely from the inside. There is a carbide lamp and matches on your table, should you wish to use it."

Miss Bristol eyed the revolver. "I am not unfamiliar with such weapons, having fired them more than a few times, my father saying it was a necessary part of my education. I am rather a good shot."

"I am not surprised in the least to hear this. Sleep well, Miss Bristol."

After Arthur had left, Miss Bristol stood outside her tent for a few minutes, gazing up at the night sky, taken aback by the astonishing tapestry of stars visible at this remote location. She could just make out the silhouette of the Pyramid of the Sun against the shimmering background of stars. It was magical, even with her understanding of science, and the physical laws which allowed stars and moons and planets to endlessly spin through the vast cosmos.

She entered her tent, tying the tent flaps securely, placing Arthur's revolver under her pillow. Arthur was right, there were a wide variety of snakes in this world, and the worst ones walked on two legs.

The laborers arrived the next morning in the horse-drawn omnibus, Arthur and Miss Bristol meeting with Ezra Crowder, showing him the map of the four proposed dig locations.

The first dig would take place along the Avenue of the Dead where a large number of ancient dwellings had previously been uncovered, unearthing a trove of artifacts used in the day-to-day life of the early Mesoamerican inhabitants. There were numerous structures in the area, however, which had not yet been excavated, and it was these which Arthur had noted on his map.

The second dig would occur beneath the Pyramid of the Sun, following a tunnel originally dug by looters in the distant past. When the looters' tunnel was being excavated in the 1880s, a man-made system of caves and tunnels lying beneath the pyramid was revealed, the central chamber being in the shape of a clover, symbolizing the underworld and the origin of life. Arthur's main focus on the second dig were two unexplored tunnels branching out from the clover-shaped central chamber, possibly part of a tunnel system leading directly to the Pyramid of the Moon.

The third dig was at a grouping of eight lesser temples near the Pyramid of the Moon, temples which had held strong religious significance to the builders of Teotihuacan. They would also excavate smaller structures surrounding the temples, more than likely used for a variety of religious rituals.

The fourth and final dig was in a tunnel that ran beneath the Pyramid of the Moon, possibly leading to a hidden chamber mentioned in Charnay's journals from 1883.

It was the second dig, beneath the Pyramid of the Sun, which occupied the most time, taking three weeks for the laborers to clear out the rubble and safely shore up portions of the ancient collapsed tunnels.

As the digging slowly progressed, Arthur and Miss Bristol carefully mapped the locations of all the artifacts they found: obsidian blades and arrowheads, intricately decorated shards of pottery, burned animal bones, a multitude of greenstone beads and figurines, and most importantly, a number of large ceramic vessels in a thirty-foot-wide chamber were found—the vessels containing numerous objects made of jade, shell, and obsidian, offerings to a variety of deities. Arthur said it was believed the primary purpose of the tunnels was for religious rituals, the tunnels possibly representing a map of the underworld. The tunnels may also have aligned with celestial events such as the positioning of the stars and planets at certain times of the year.

The excavation itself was slow going, Arthur taking great care to make certain that nothing was damaged or misplaced, Miss Bristol mapping out the tunnel and chambers in the minutest detail, creating detailed lists and descriptions of the artifacts they found.

It took almost a month to make their way through over five hundred feet of the tunnel, Arthur certain it was making a direct line to the Pyramid of the Moon. He ordered the excavation to be halted when they reached a section of the tunnel which was blocked by massive carved slabs of stone placed there by the original inhabitants of Teotihuacan, traces of colored pigment still remaining on the surface of the gargantuan stones. He was uncertain of the purpose or symbology of the stones, and why they had been placed their to block the path of the tunnel, but it brought an end to the dig. He suspected the massive blocks of stone may have been placed there to deter looters from robbing the offerings made to the deities which lay hidden beneath the pyramids.

During the digs, George spent most of his time

above ground, exploring Teotihuacan and taking numerous photographs with his camera, most notably at the Ciudadela, a massive enclosure with ceremonial and political significance, a number of underground tunnels having been discovered beneath it. Most importantly, it held the Temple of Quetzalcoatl, the feathered serpent deity. As the days passed, George made certain his explorations brought him closer and closer to the location of the tunnel entrance discovered by Frederick Beaumont, strolling past it several times. He drew his own maps, making sure Ezra Crowder saw his drawings—the maps revealing nothing of the expedition's hidden purpose.

Numerous other excavations had previously taken place within the Ciudadela, including the discovery of a tunnel running beneath The Temple of the Feathered Serpent which led to a large chamber filled with thousands of artifacts, including figurines, jade, and even liquid mercury—possibly used to symbolize a mythical underworld river.

Miss Bristol had brought with her several dozen maps and journals recounting the findings of the anthropologists who came before them. After careful examination she had found that none of the journals referenced the entrance to Beaumont's tunnel. In truth, the extent of the mysterious tunnel system which ran beneath Teotihuacan was largely unknown, although it was believed that a number of large undiscovered chambers and natural caverns more than likely lay beneath the pyramids.

After six weeks at Teotihuacan, Miss Bristol casually approached the location of the entrance to Beaumont's tunnel, noting a circular twelve-foot-wide mound of earth, no more than a foot or two high, covered with low thorny shrubs. Before they could begin digging, Miss Bristol knew they needed a reason to excavate there, something which would not arouse the suspicions of their foreman.

After some discussion that evening with Arthur and George, the three friends hatched their plan. Arthur would go out under cover of darkness and bury a small clay pot in the mound, the rim of the pot barely visible above the surface of the ground, doing his best to make the area appear undisturbed, as though the pot had been there for centuries.

The following day, Miss Bristol asked Ezra if she could borrow a small shovel to dig up a clay pot she had noticed on her morning walk. As she had expected, Ezra sent two laborers to the location, carefully digging up what Arthur had so recently buried. Miss Bristol suggested they dig deeper, noting that more artifacts might be buried at that location.

The digging stopped when their shovels uncovered a number of heavy wooden beams, Miss Bristol calling Arthur and George to the site, Ezra also making an appearance.

They decided to move the large timbers, hoping to discover the reason for their presence. The three friends feigned surprise when it was revealed that the heavy timbers had been covering a large hole, a shaft dropping down over twenty feet into an apparently unexplored tunnel.

Ezra had the workers build a tall wooden ladder, allowing the three friends to descend into the tunnel, warning them to keep an eye out for scorpions and several known varieties of poisonous spiders which might be inhabiting the tunnel.

Among the excavation supplies they had brought with them were six carbide lamps, which they had been using in the tunnels beneath the Pyramid of the Sun. Arthur opened a pouch containing calcium carbide pellets, dropping them into three of the lanterns, then poured in a small amount of water, waiting for the hissing sound of acetylene gas as the water dripped slowly onto the calcium carbide pellets. Striking a wooden match, he lit the three lanterns, a brilliant white flame appearing. He handed lamps to Miss Bristol and George.

The workers held the ladder securely in place as the three friends descended into the tunnel, greeted by the musty smell of earth and ancient decay.

The tunnel was almost six feet tall and six feet wide, allowing them to walk without hunching over, something which pleased Miss Bristol greatly.

George whispered, “Which way?”

Miss Bristol studied the small brass compass in her hand, pointing to the east. She held up her lamp, peering down the shadowy tunnel. “This is the direction indicated in Beaumont’s map.”

Arthur climbed up the ladder, calling out to Ezra, “The tunnel looks clear as far as we can see, but we shall return if we reach a section which has collapsed.”

“I will have two workers wait here until we hear from you. Take great care, the tunnels can be hazardous—more than one explorer has lost their life to a sudden collapse.”

“We shall take no chances, you may be assured of that.”

Arthur climbed back down into the tunnel and they made their way forward, holding up the bright hissing carbide lamps to illuminate the way. Miss Bristol stopped after a few yards, running her hand along the tunnel wall. “Do the walls seem unusually smooth to you?"

Arthur nodded, "They are smooth, far smoother than the tunnels beneath Pyramids of the Sun and Moon, but perhaps for some reason they simply took great care in digging this particular tunnel."

George said, "Or perhaps it was someone else who dug the tunnel."

Arthur laughed. "I have no idea to whom you may be referring."

"Those green fellows with the enormous heads and six black eyes?"

Miss Bristol laughed. "They sound quite frightening."

They continued on for ten minutes, carefully examining the tunnel walls and floor, searching for relics, finding none, their lamps casting long shadows across the tunnel walls. The tunnel curved slightly to the right, sloping down sharply, the three of them stopping after twenty feet when they saw the mound of earth and stone ahead of them, partially blocking the tunnel.

Arthur stepped closer, examining the collapsed section of tunnel, pointing to a two-foot-wide opening at the top of the rubble. "We can quite easily fit through there. There is no need to clear away the entire blockage."

George climbed up to the dark opening, holding his lamp next to it. “I can see through, we shall only have to crawl four or five feet to reach the other side.”

George went first, holding the bright carbide lamp in front of him as he crawled cautiously through the opening, calling out to them when he had clambered down into the next section of the tunnel. “You may come through, the tunnel appears to be safe, with no collapses ahead that I can see. It continues to descend at a steep angle.”

Miss Bristol’s trepidation rose as she approached the narrow entryway, fighting the urge to voice her fears that the tunnel might collapse as she was crawling through the opening. She also recognized that if she was going to have a career in anthropology she must overcome her fear of confined spaces. This thought gave her the impetus she needed to continue on. Three minutes later she was standing next to Arthur and George, brushing the dirt and dust from her hair.

George said, “Did Beaumont note how far he had traveled down the tunnel before he found the fabric sleeve, or how far beneath the surface he was when he found it?”

“He did not. His notation regarding the fabric appears to have been an afterthought, as he clearly did not recognize its significance. It is possible he simply thought it to be a piece of cloth left by an earlier expedition. I don't believe he went a great distance, or he certainly would have mentioned it in his notes. He did say he stopped at a tunnel collapse, but there could be more than one."

"Is it curious that we have found no artifacts within the tunnel?"

Arthur nodded. "It is quite curious. It is also curious that there are no images painted on the tunnel walls. It is possible that this may have been a looters' tunnel, an attempt to locate chambers beneath the Temple of the Feathered Serpent."

They continued on, making their way through the murky passage, Miss Bristol commenting several more times on the smoothness of the walls.

After another thirty yards, Arthur stopped, holding his lantern up. "There is another collapse ahead of us."

They cautiously approached it, shining their lamps on the roof of the tunnel. Miss Bristol searched for any possible openings which would allow them to pass through the wall of stone and earth, but found none. "I fear we have reached an impasse. This may have been the point where Beaumont stopped."

George said, "Should we go back and call in the

laborers to remove the rubble?"

Arthur thought for a minute, then said, "The less they see of this tunnel, the better it shall be for us. Miss Bristol is quite right, there is something unusual about the tunnel's construction, and I have no desire to arouse Mr. Crowder's curiosity."

"What shall we do?"

"Let us attempt to clear away enough of the debris that we can pass through."

"It will not collapse further?"

Arthur pulled a small folding shovel from his pack. "If we are careful, and gently remove debris from the top of the mound, we should be quite safe."

The blockage proved to be less of an obstacle than they had initially feared, taking only twenty minutes to create an opening large enough for them to crawl through.

Arthur was the first one to reach the other side of the blockage, holding his lamp up, his eyes widening at the sight of the circular chamber lying ahead of them. Miss Bristol came through next, stopping short when she saw the chamber.

"What is this? It does not look like any of the other chambers we have seen in the tunnels."

George clambered down the pile of rubble, his eyes on the chamber. "This is a sight, the chamber forms a perfect hemisphere, at least thirty feet tall, a dome, the walls like polished glass."

Arthur ran his hand across the smooth chamber wall. "This was not created by the Aztecs or the Mesoamericans who first inhabited Teotihuacan, of that I am certain. I have never seen walls such as this, made of smooth gleaming glass. There are no artifacts to be found, and no decorative paintings or carvings on the chamber walls."

George squinted, shielding his eyes from his carbide lamp. "Are my eyes deceiving me, or is the chamber glowing slightly?"

The three of them shut off their carbide lamps, their eyes on the softly glowing walls of the glass dome.

"Your eyes were not deceiving you. The walls and ceiling are glowing with a curious light, especially that circular area in the center of the floor."

George stepped over to the center of the dome, eyeing the six-foot-wide circular glowing area. "What do you suppose it is for? The light within the circle is not constant, it seems to be pulsating gently."

Arthur shook his head. "This is far beyond my understanding."

Miss Bristol gazed up at the ceiling, furrowing her brow. "Are those stars?"

Chapter 16

Arthur looked up, studying the thousands of barely visible flickering points of light on the ceiling. "I see no recognizable constellations, but they do look like stars."

Miss Bristol said, "How strange, when I look at a particular star, its brightness increases. It is a most peculiar sensation."

Arthur and George gazed up at the stars, Arthur saying, "You are quite right, Miss Bristol, my gaze does indeed affect the brightness of any star I focus on." Arthur stepped into the circular section of light, continuing to gaze at single star, its light growing brighter and brighter, Miss Bristol shielding her eyes.

"Stop! We have no idea what the purpose the stars might have, or if they are stars. It might be something else entirely, something dangerous."

Arthur looked away, the brilliant blazing star returning to a pinpoint of flickering light.

"Whatever it is, it was not created by man."

"What could the purpose of such a thing possibly be?"

Miss Bristol rubbed her chin. "It must fulfill a need for them. Perhaps the beings feed on light. Perhaps they absorb the light of the star they are looking at, just as the fabric absorbed the energy of the dagger and the bullet."

George gave a dubious look. "They use light to create food energy in the same fashion as plants? If this was so, why would they create a subterranean tunnel?"

"I have no idea what they were doing down here or what they were looking for."

Arthur said, "Whatever the purpose of the stars, it is the final proof we need that the tunnel was not created by the inhabitants of Teotihuacan."

Miss Bristol nodded. "We are getting close, I can feel it in my bones."

They lit their carbide lamps again, Arthur pointing to the far side of the glowing dome. "The tunnel continues on."

They crossed to the other side of the chamber, stepping into the tunnel, stopping after ten feet, George holding up his lantern. "The tunnel has collapsed again."

"It is unlike the other collapses we have seen."

George nodded his agreement. "It looks as if the walls have melted, liquid rock running down the sides, perhaps causing the roof of the tunnel to collapse. Could it have been lava?"

Arthur shook his head. "The tunnel is not a lava tube such as those left after volcanic eruptions. There is some other unknown force at work here, something which caused the rock to melt, the tunnel to collapse."

Miss Bristol walked over to the wall of stone and earth. "The melted rock walls are smooth and glass-like, similar to the walls of the chamber." She gave a sudden start, stepping back quickly, pointing to some unknown object.

"What is it, what have you found?"

"There are bones protruding from the rubble. It appears to be a human hand."

Arthur stepped over to Miss Bristol, kneeling down, examining the bones. "You are correct in your assumption that the bones belong to a hand, but it is most assuredly not a human hand."

"How can you be certain?"

"There are six fingers, each finger composed of four segments, not three, as in humans. Also, the bones are connected by some form of organic material which has not deteriorated with time. In humans, the bones are connected by cartilage and muscle, something which deteriorates, the individual bones becoming disconnected, separating. These bones remain connected."

Miss Bristol's voice was almost a whisper. "We have found one of them, one of the beings who visited our world?"

"It would appear so, Miss Bristol. We must clear away the debris to examine it further."

Miss Bristol kneeled down, removing handfuls of small rocks, brushing away the earth with a soft bristle brush, stopping when she saw the pale gray fabric. "It's the same fabric. We have found them."

Arthur and George crouched down next her, Arthur studying the fabric that encircled the creature's arm like a sleeve. "It does resemble the fabric that Beaumont found."

George grabbed a corner of it, stretching it out almost eighteen inches before releasing it, the fabric snapping back to its original size. "There is no doubt that this is the same fabric. Miss Bristol is right, we have found one of the visitors." He grabbed a shovel. "We need to dig it up."

"Not now. It will take time to properly excavate the skeleton. We must not forget that this is an archeological dig, not a treasure hunt. Besides, Crowder's men are waiting for us. We should leave, tell them we found nothing, that the tunnel was unfinished, most likely a looter's tunnel."

"And what then?"

"We shall return at night, under cover of darkness, while the laborers and Mr. Crowder are sleeping."

George grinned. "That shall be an adventure to remember, skulking about in the dark of night like a trio of nefarious sneak thieves."

Miss Bristol's eyes were still on the six-fingered hand. "It is hard to believe what I am seeing—a being from beyond the stars, from a distant world."

When they emerged from the tunnel they did their best to appear disappointed, Arthur saying, "There was nothing to be found, no artifacts. I'm quite certain it was an unfinished tunnel dug by looters attempting to rob offerings hidden beneath the Temple of the Feathered Serpent."

They covered the entrance with the heavy timbers, heading back to their tents.

Two nights later, Miss Bristol crept silently out of her tent, a partial moon illuminating the landscape just enough for the three friends to find their way along the Avenue of the Dead without the aid of their carbide lamps. They walked silently toward the Ciudadela, then past The Temple of the Feathered Serpent, finally arriving at the tunnel entrance, carefully moving to one side the heavy wooden beams that covered the hole.

Arthur said, "The ladder is still in place. I'll go first." He climbed down the ladder, moving a few yards down the tunnel, then stopped to light a carbide lamp.

Miss Bristol came down next, then George. Arthur handed each of them a lamp. "We must hurry."

They headed down the tunnel as quickly as they could, crawling through the first opening. When they reached the second tunnel collapse, they scrambled through the narrow entrance they had previously cleared, climbing down into the dome-shaped glass chamber.

Arthur pointed to the far side of the chamber. "That way."

They darted across the glowing chamber floor, stepping into the collapsed tunnel, Miss Bristol's eyes on the curiously melted rock and the bony hand protruding from the rubble.

George pulled two small folding shovels from his pack, handing one to Arthur. "Miss Bristol, if you would like to hold the lantern, we shall begin the excavation of our otherworldly visitor."

They gently dug away at the mound of rocks and debris, Miss Bristol watching as the creature's form was slowly revealed.

Arthur pulled a heavy rock to one side, giving a shout, “A second skeleton! There are two of them!”

Two more hours passed before the two skeletons were fully revealed, the three friends kneeling down next to them, using soft bristle brushes to clear away the dust and dirt from the bones and the mysterious fabric.

“They are at least seven feet tall, I would say.”

Miss Bristol ran her hand across one of the skulls. “Their skulls are of a reptilian form, resembling a large lizard, or a small crocodile.”

“They have enormous eye sockets.”

Miss Bristol shivered. “They must have been frightening creatures to behold, with their lizard heads and immense eyes.”

Arthur shrugged. “Perhaps they would have said the same of us, with our curiously rounded heads and small beady eyes.”

Miss Bristol laughed. “I have never thought of myself as having small beady eyes.”

George turned one of the skulls gently. “Whatever their appearance, they had to have been creatures of great intellect to devise a ship which could cross the infinitely vast expanses of empty space.”

Arthur nodded his agreement. “Well said, sir, and

quite true. We must not judge them by their appearance."

"They are both wearing suits made of the fabric we found. It should have protected them from the falling rocks, prevented any injuries."

Arthur said, "Their torsos were most probably unharmed by the falling rocks, but their heads were not. There is a crack in the top of this skull, most likely from a heavy falling rock. Even if they were uninjured by the collapse, they would have been trapped beneath the rubble, unable to free themselves. They would have suffocated, or worse, died of thirst or starvation."

Miss Bristol grimaced. "What a dreadful way to die, so far from their home, on a strange, distant world."

"They are both wearing heavy belts around their waists. Let's turn them over."

They gently rolled the first skeleton onto its back, Arthur noting two rows of indecipherable symbols on its clothing. "This must be their written language. It is most curious, some form of hieroglyph perhaps."

George said, "On his belt, is that a weapon? It looks like a holstered pistol of some kind."

Arthur reached over to the holster, gently removing the curious device. "It most certainly does look like a weapon."

George grinned. "What do you suppose it does?"

Miss Bristol frowned. "Be careful with it. It could be extremely dangerous, and we have no idea how it works. There is a chance it might not be a weapon at all, perhaps it is a tool they were using to melt the rock."

"That might well explain the smooth glass walls of the chamber, but not the stars on the ceiling."

"This one has what looks like a hollow ring of blue glass in its hand, but it has been smashed to bits by the rocks."

George reached across to a square pouch on the creature's belt, gently removing two rectangular crystalline containers, each holding nine silver cylinders approximately two inches long and a half-inch wide. One end of each cylinder was dome-shaped, composed of a bright green, translucent, glass-like material.

"Is this ammunition for the weapon? Are they bullets?"

"I don't know, perhaps."

Arthur moved closer to the carbide lamp, examining the pistol under the bright light, turning it over slowly. "The grip is meant to fit their hands, slightly larger than ours. There are a number of small hieroglyphs imprinted on the barrel of the device. There is a wide cylindrical barrel, but it appears to be solid, composed of the green glass-like substance, with a white cylindrical core running through the center of it. The material is similar in nature to the rounded ends of the small silver cylinders. There is a rounded protrusion at the back of the trigger guard, but there is no trigger."

"Perhaps you press the round button to fire the weapon."

"Perhaps. Look here, at the bottom of the grip—one of those small cylinders has been inserted into a circular hole."

"If the cylinders are placed in the grip, then they are not bullets as we understand them."

"It must power the weapon somehow, charging it, perhaps allowing it to project energy beams?"

George's eyes were bright. "Are you suggesting they are death rays, like those used by the Martians in *War of the Worlds*?"

"Anything is possible, I suppose."

Arthur eyed a small tab on the back of the weapon's grip. "This appears to be a button or a switch of some kind." He tentatively pressed it, almost dropping the weapon when the barrel took on a green glow, the device making a low humming sound.

"Good heavens, the device is still functional." He pressed the tab again, the humming sound stopping, the barrel becoming dark again. "The weapon is activated by the round button on the back of the grip."

George said, "The question is, once the gun has been activated, what happens when the trigger button is pressed?"

"This is not the time or place to determine that."

"A rather mercenary thought just occurred to me—if it is a death ray, or some other form of deadly weapon, can you possibly conceive of how much money the military would pay us for such a device? We would be wealthy beyond measure."

Arthur turned to George. "You surprise me, sir. If, in fact, this is a weapon similar to those written about by H.G. Wells, a heat ray, or a death ray, the very last people who should know about it are the military forces of this world. Surely you have read about John Browning's machine gun which fires over four hundred rounds per minute? It is madness to have such deadly weapons as that. I would not give them a death ray if my very life depended on it; I would destroy it first. Humanity is not ready for such weaponry as that."

"What you say is quite true, but consider this: with such a weapon in the hands of all armies, would it not spell the end to all wars, the consequences of any such conflict being too terrible to imagine?"

"I fear you have more faith in man's innate good nature than I. There are despots who place little value on human lives. Either way, this is not a decision we must make now, as we have no idea the purpose of these devices. Perhaps they are nothing more than bright lights used to illuminate the tunnels."

They rolled the second creature over, finding another holstered weapon and two crystalline boxes of the silver charging cylinders.

"Should we dig further? Perhaps there are more of them, more curious devices, possibly still functional."

"We have discovered enough for now. We can return later if we choose. We are running out of time."

"What about the skeletons? Should we do something with them?"

Arthur shook his head. "Not now, I fear the resulting consequences if the presence of otherworldly creatures were to become common knowledge. There could be widespread panic and chaos across the globe."

Miss Bristol said, "Perhaps we could take several of the bones back with us, examining them in the laboratory. The skulls are fascinating. It would appear that reptiles, rather than mammals, were the intelligent species of their world."

"We can make future plans back at the tent. We must head back now, we have been here for over four hours, and the laborers will be awakening soon, preparing for the day's work. I do not wish them to see us emerging from the tunnel."

Arthur handed one of the weapons and its charging cylinders to George, and one to Miss Bristol. "Keep these hidden. It must be said again; no one must learn of our discoveries here—it could bring absolute chaos to the world. We will bring the weapons back to New York with us, testing them at a safe and secure location, discovering their purpose."

They packed up their gear, heading back through the tunnel, arriving at their camp just in time to see the faint orange glow of sunrise peeking above the eastern horizon.

The following day, Miss Bristol could scarcely keep her eyes open as they stood at their excavation site near the The Pyramid of the Moon, something which did not go unnoticed by Ezra Crowder.

"You look quite tired, Miss Bristol, are you not sleeping well? Is it the heat of the day which tires you?"

"It is of my own doing, Mr. Crowder. I stayed up half the night reading the journals of archeologists who have visited Teotihuacan in the past. It makes quite fascinating reading, learning of their discoveries."

"Of course, I understand." He smiled at Miss Bristol, but it was a smile that sent shivers down her spine.

George glanced over at Arthur, who was pointing to a shiny black object protruding from the ground. "There, an obsidian knife blade."

The final excavation was in a tunnel beneath the Pyramid of the Moon, lasting for over a month, their progress slowed considerably by the collapse of a section of tunnel, one of the laborers badly injured, his leg broken. As luck would have it, a carriage bringing provisions was arriving the next day, the injured worker returning with the carriage to Mexico City.

When the collapse was cleared away, they continued down the tunnel, discovering a large chamber, a natural cave formation, the walls covered with faded paintings of various deities, and three large ceramic pots filled with offerings to the gods.

Arthur suspected the offerings were for a deity known as the Teotihuacan Great Goddess, noting the images on the wall of a woman wearing a bird headdress, a spider motif radiating out from her body. He believed her to be a goddess of water and fertility, but it was more of an educated guess, the paintings having been there prior to the arrival of the Aztecs at Teotihuacan.

The dig provided them with dozens of fascinating artifacts to bring back with them—artifacts which would most certainly please Dr. Boas.

When the dig beneath the Pyramid of the Moon had reached its conclusion, the tunnel was carefully sealed, and the artifacts taken back to the tents to be safely packed in straw, then secured in wooden crates.

As they were making their way back to the camp, Arthur approached Mr. Crowder, saying, "As you know, our time here at Teotihuacan is drawing to a close. Our train leaves Mexico City in five days, our steamship departing from Veracruz two days later."

Mr. Crowder nodded. "Of course. We have already packed most of the artifacts for your trip back to New York. I trust you have been satisfied with my services, and the work of the laborers?"

"You have been marvelous, sir, as have the workers. We could not have asked for a better foreman. Everything went smoothly, and we are more than pleased with both the artifacts we have found and with the amount of knowledge we have gained about Teotihuacan. Many of the artifacts shall be donated to the American Museum of Natural History in New York, once they have been carefully studied. They shall be viewed and appreciated by thousands of visitors every year."

Mr. Crowder gave a slight bow. "I have myself visited the museum on several occasions."

Miss Bristol was silent, her eyes fixed on Mr. Crowder. She did not like the look in his eyes.

Chapter 17

The next day was spent packing the remaining artifacts in straw, placing them carefully into the large wooden crates for shipping. Arthur had the workers seal the entrance to Beaumont's tunnel, placing several feet of earth on top of the wooden beams covering the entrance. Perhaps one day they would return to further excavate the tunnel, looking for other objects left by the visitors.

The following morning Miss Bristol rose with the sun, dressing quickly, surveying her tent. She was going to miss the sense of adventure she found here, the excitement of finding ancient artifacts which hadn't been seen in two thousand years, but she was also ready to return to New York.

There was much to do before they left, most importantly, sealing the tunnel entrance at the Pyramid of the Sun, something which would take at least half a day. After that had been done, she would return to her tent, organizing and packing her belongings. She picked up several journals, setting them in her steamer trunk, then stopped abruptly, tilting her head. Something was not right, but it took her a moment to realize what it was. It was the stillness, the eerie silence.

Arthur and George had already stepped out of their tent, George looking toward the laborers' campsite. "That's odd, the workers have not risen yet. They are normally having their breakfast by this time, milling about, preparing for the day's work."

"That is odd indeed. Where could they be?"

Mr. Crowder's voice sounded from behind them. "I have sent the workers home, back to the city. I told them their work here was done."

Arthur turned to face him. "Are we not returning to the Pyramid of the Sun today, sealing the tunnel?"

"We are not. I took it upon myself to pay the laborers a few dollars to leave early."

"Why on earth would you do that?"

Mr. Crowder smiled, pulling a black revolver from his pocket, pointing it at Arthur and George. "I sent them back because it is my intention to rob you of the treasure you found in your secret tunnel."

Arthur gave him a puzzled look. "I have no idea what you mean, sir. We found no treasure. As we already told you, there was nothing to be found in the tunnel, not even an arrowhead, there was nothing. It was an unfinished tunnel dug by unsuccessful looters." His hand pressed against his hip, feeling for the Webley, but it was in the tent.

"You are a most accomplished liar. I might even have believed you if one of my men had not seen you leaving your campsite in the dead of night, the very same night that Miss Bristol said she had been reading journals in her tent. Strangely enough, there was no light coming from her tent that night. Can Miss Bristol read in the dark?"

Crowder's revolver had not moved, it was still aimed directly at Arthur and George.

"We have no treasure, sir. We found nothing in the tunnel."

"The laborer thinks you found gold and jewels from an unknown burial site. He claims to have seen you carrying something shiny that sparkled in the moonlight."

"He is wrong, we found nothing. I swear to you that we found no gold or jewels."

"Enough of your lies. You visited the tunnel in the darkness of night to remove treasure from a hidden chamber. You will bring me the treasure or you shall both die where you stand. You have no other choice. It is quite simple—even a person without a degree from your great Columbia University could understand it."

"There is no treasure to be had, sir."

Mr. Crowder raised the pistol, aiming it at Arthur. "Perhaps if I kill one of you, that will be enough for the other one to do as I ask."

A voice sounded from Miss Bristol's tent. "Do not shoot them. I have the treasure. I will give it to you gladly if you spare their lives. Its value is beyond measure."

Crowder gave a cold smile. "Much better." He called out to Miss Bristol, "Bring it to me or your friends shall die."

Miss Bristol stepped out of her tent, a wooden box in one hand, the other hand behind her back. She stepped over to Arthur and George, setting the box on the ground in front of her.

Crowder said, "What is in the box?"

"Gold chains and pendants, gemstones, three golden jeweled daggers."

He aimed his pistol at her. "Step back, all of you."

The three of them moved away from the box, Crowder approaching it, kneeling down, his revolver still aimed at them. He lowered it for a moment as he attempted to open the box, Miss Bristol's arm swinging out in front of her, her voice as cold as ice. "Do not move, drop your weapon."

Crowder looked up in surprise, seeing the ancient otherworldly weapon gripped in her hand, the barrel glowing with a pale green light, a barely audible humming sound filling the air. The weapon was pointed directly at Mr. Crowder, Miss Bristol's finger on the rounded protrusion beneath the trigger guard.

Crowder gave a start when he saw the weapon, a momentary fear flickering across his face. "What is that?"

"You will take your leave, sir, and not return. Drop your weapon"

Crowder gave a sudden derisive laugh. "It is a child's toy, brandished by a silly little girl." He flipped the lid of the box open. It was empty. His eyes went cold, a chilling smile appearing on his face. "Very clever, the box is empty. I shall kill all of you now and take the treasure myself." He slowly raised his pistol, the chilling smile still on his face.

Mr. Crowder had unwittingly made the gravest error in judgement he could possibly have made when he called Miss Bristol a silly little girl.

Time seemed to slow down for Miss Bristol as she watched Crowder raising the revolver. She knew there were moments in life when everything changes in an instant, when life as we know it is turned upside down: a tragic accident, somber words from a doctor, an unexpected visit from a police officer, a distressing letter from a dear old friend. She also knew that she was about to experience one of those moments.

As Crowder raised his revolver, Miss Bristol pressed the firing tab on the curious weapon, the words *silly little girl* still ringing in her ears.

A blinding beam of white light shot out from the weapon, a thousand wriggling oblong green glowing bubbles streaming behind it, the beam of light striking Mr. Crowder directly on his chest, a look of stunned surprise appearing on his face, his smirk vanishing, his gun falling to the ground. Surprise turned to terror as he watched the green bubbles rapidly coalesce around him, enveloping him in a single large shimmering bubble. He pushed wildly against the undulating bubble walls, trying to free himself from this quivering otherworldly prison, but his efforts in this endeavor proved to be quite unsuccessful.

It was over in less than a second, Mr. Crowder vanishing in a brilliant flash of white light, the large green bubble fading away to nothingness.

The silence was almost unbearable, the three friends staring at the spot where Mr. Crowder had once stood with his pistol aimed directly at them.

Miss Bristol lowered the weapon, her voice a whisper. "I have killed him. I have killed Mr. Crowder. I am a murderer."

Arthur quickly stepped over to her, gently taking the weapon from her hands, deactivating it.

"It is not your fault, you are not to blame. It was Mr. Crowder's own actions which ended his life—he was the architect of his own demise, not you. You are a hero, Miss Bristol; you saved our lives today with your quick thinking and your bravery."

"I killed him."

Arthur put his hand on Miss Bristol's arm. "You saved our lives."

"What should we do? Should we contact the authorities and tell them what has happened?"

"What would you tell them, that Mr. Crowder vanished when you shot him with a weapon brought here by visitors from beyond the stars, from a distant world, another galaxy?"

"They would not believe me."

George said, "They most certainly would not. Not to be overly pragmatic, but there is no body to be found, no proof that anything ever happened here. As far as we know, Mr. Crowder simply returned to his home in Mexico City at the conclusion of the dig."

Arthur said, "George is quite right. The omnibus will be here in two days to pick us up and take us to Mexico City. Our train leaves for Veracruz the next day, the *SS Merida* sailing the day after our arrival. When that day comes, we shall be safely aboard the *SS Merida*, on our way back to New York."

"I shall live with this guilt for the rest of my days."

Arthur said, "Your remorse tells me what I already knew, Miss Bristol, that you are a kind person who wishes no harm visited upon anyone. It also tells me you have a hidden strength within you, the strength to do what was necessary to save our lives."

"I was filled with such dreadful anger when he called me a silly little girl."

"You are anything but that, Miss Bristol."

George smiled. "A fact that Mr. Crowder is now well aware of." His eyes were fixed on the weapon in Arthur's hand.

They spent the rest of the morning packing their personal belongings into their steamer trunks, then moved on to the gargantuan task of taking down all the tents and returning them to their packing crates, preparing the folding cots and tables for the journey home.

George said, "We shall have to sleep under the stars tonight, hopefully not to be eaten by a coyote, or one of those deadly looking armadillo creatures."

Arthur laughed. "Armadillos are quite harmless. I would recommend directing your fears toward something more appropriate, such as rattlesnakes and scorpions, for example."

Miss Bristol frowned. "We must keep watch, each of us taking a turn while the others sleep. It is possible that Mr. Crowder had unknown accomplices who might be looking for him, might be wondering what has happened to him."

George's smile vanished. "You make a good point, Miss Bristol. We shall sleep in shifts, using the six carbide lamps to frighten away any nocturnal creatures."

Arthur said, "We shall also keep the Webley .455 at the ready."

George nodded. "At least now we know the purpose of the weapon we found. It is a death ray, as we suspected."

Arthur looked uncertain. "Perhaps it is so, but I am at a loss to explain the green bubble which surrounded Mr. Crowder. What was the purpose of it? Why not simply a beam of white hot light that would…"

"Burn a hole in him?"

"Precisely, as dreadful as it sounds. Much like a bullet made of light."

George shrugged. "Perhaps it is a simple way to dispose of the body. I am afraid I have no other answers to give you. All I know is that Crowder was here, and then he was not. Perhaps when the visitors return we shall be able to ask them about the purpose of the green bubbles."

"Meeting them is a thought which is both intriguing and terrifying. I would hope that H.G. Wells was wrong about the nature of such visitors, that they would have evolved beyond brutality."

Miss Bristol said, "If you think about it logically, what could we possibly have that they would want? Would they come from beyond the stars to steal our telegraphs and light bulbs and aeroplanes? They can visit any world they wish in this infinitely vast universe. I feel quite certain they should think us to be nothing more than primitive savages at best. Perhaps they would study us in the same fashion that a biologist studies frogs in a pond."

Arthur said, "It was not so long ago that we were primitive savages."

"Perhaps in another hundred thousand years we shall have changed our ways, become a race of peaceful beings, putting an end to the senseless wars we wage against each other."

"I hope you are right, Miss Bristol. Until that day comes, we must retain our faith in humanity. There is always hope."

Two days later the omnibus arrived, along with

heavy wagons to carry their expedition supplies and crates of artifacts back to Mexico City.

Six days later, the early morning sun found Miss Bristol standing on the *SS Merida's* second-class promenade, gazing out across the ocean, her thoughts returning to the untimely demise of Mr. Crowder. She knew he would have taken their lives and thought nothing of it, so why was she so profoundly affected by what she had done? There were times when she wished her conscience would not torment her so, commenting on her every action, her every decision, her every word. A question still plagued her—would she have killed Crowder if he had not called her a silly little girl? Was it her anger at the personal insult that had caused her to take his life?

"I trust you slept well, Miss Bristol?"

She turned to see Arthur standing next to her, his presence having become a most welcome sight. "Yes, quite well, thank you, Arthur. I believe the sea air does me good."

"From the look on your face, I suspect you are still pondering the events of eight days ago?"

"I will confess I am still deeply troubled by them."

"Perhaps one day you will come to understand the reason for those events and forgive yourself."

"Are you a religious man, Arthur?"

"I am not sure that is the adjective I would use, but I believe there is a reason for every event, a valuable lesson to be learned from the trials we face. I also believe that we draw such lessons to us as are necessary, both through events and the people we meet. Some would call it fate, but as they say, a rose by any other name would smell as sweet."

"And what do you suppose I should learn from such an event as the one eight days ago?"

"Perhaps it is not what you think you are meant to learn, perhaps it is something else entirely. Perhaps you are meant to learn forgiveness, Miss Bristol—not of others, but of yourself. Fate gave you no choice in the matter, and there is a reason for that. We would not be here discussing this if you had done otherwise. If fate had wished for your life to end, it would have been so, Crowder would have killed us all without a thought. We are still alive in this world for a reason, we still have purpose."

"I do hope you are right, Arthur." She thought for a moment, then said, "Arthur, I should like you to know that your kindness and your reassuring comments are a soothing balm to my troubled thoughts. I am most grateful for them."

"I'm glad to hear this, Miss Bristol. You do not deserve to be so tormented by these events. You saved my life, and for that you have my eternal gratitude."

"Again, I thank you."

"Are you looking forward to our return?"

"I have never seen such sights as I have on this expedition, but I do look forward to a return to familiarity, to the comforts of my home, to seeing my parents again, to strolling across the campus on a sunny day."

"I would heartily agree; it will be good to return to a daily routine. I only hope Dr. Boas is pleased with our efforts."

"Three large crates of marvelous artifacts should certainly be enough to please him."

"There is always hope, Miss Bristol."

"And the objects we recovered from Beaumont's tunnel? What shall become of them?"

"I would ask you to place yours in a safe and secure place where it will not accidentally be discovered. I also would ask you not to tell me or George where you have hidden them. As for the objects in George's possession, when the time is right they shall be examined carefully, and a decision made whether or not to destroy them."

"If I may be quite forthcoming, I do not believe George will choose to destroy them."

Arthur gave a sigh. "I understand your concern, and I thank you for your candor, Miss Bristol. I'm afraid George will have to learn a difficult lesson—that there are things in this world far more important than our own personal desires. No matter how wealthy it would make us, these objects must not fall into the hands of people who would misuse them."

"I agree completely."

Arthur studied Miss Bristol's face. "Then we are of one mind, Miss Bristol?"

"We are of one mind, Arthur."

Arthur was silent for a minute, gazing out across the rolling sea, Miss Bristol's eyes upon him.

Finally he said, "I suppose we should go have our lunch. I believe George is waiting for us."

"That sounds delightful, I am quite famished."

"I imagine you shall soon be calling me Professor Hollingsworth again?"

"Is that your wish, Arthur?"

"I will confess that it is most decidedly not my wish, Miss Bristol, but it is what our positions at the university demand of us."

Miss Bristol nodded. "Then it shall be so."

The *SS Merida* docked at Pier 14 seven days later, the trip proving uneventful, save for one brief violent squall, Miss Bristol pleased to discover that, unlike the first storm they had encountered, she suffered no ill effects from the rocking motion of the ship.

Chapter 18

The following Monday found Miss Bristol once again dressed in a crisp white blouse with high laced collar, black satin bow tie, and a long, flared skirt, as she strode across the campus toward Schermerhorn Hall.

As she was walking down the hallway toward the main office, she spotted Arthur stepping out of Dr. Boas' office, closing the door behind him. She waved to him. "Good morning, Professor."

He approached her, lowering his voice. "I have just met with Dr. Boas at length, discussing with him our findings at Teotihuacan."

"What did he say? Was he pleased?"

"He was very pleased indeed. He even mentioned the possibility of future expeditions. He was most impressed with your performance, how well everything was organized, the expedition running like clockwork."

"That's wonderful news."

"There is more good news, Miss Bristol. He said that although you are unable to receive a degree from the college, he is preparing to present you with an honorary degree in anthropology at the end of the fall semester, the first one he has presented to a woman. He made glowing comments regarding the maps you had drawn of the dig sites, appearing most impressed by the detail of them and with your knowledge of the artifacts."

Miss Bristol almost grabbed Arthur's arm in her excitement. "This is true, those were his exact words? I shall get an honorary degree at the end of this semester?"

"Those were his exact words. I told him you were an invaluable member of the expedition. You deserve far more than an honorary degree, but such are the times we live in. One day it will not be so."

"That is so kind of you, Arthur." She put her hand over her mouth. "I meant to say Professor Hollingsworth."

Arthur laughed. "You have not offended me in the least, Miss Bristol."

A week later, George strolled into the anthropology department, spotting Arthur and Miss Bristol chatting in the hallway.

"There they are, my two intrepid traveling

companions."

Arthur turned at the sound of George's voice. "It is a pleasure to see you, Professor Wexley. I trust you are doing well?"

"Quite well, thank you, sir. And you are also doing well?"

"I am indeed. It is good to be back in a routine again. What brings you here on this fine day?"

"I have a hypothetical question for you."

"Of course, I shall do my best to answer it."

"Let us say I had in my possession a curious artifact given to me by my father, but no idea where it came from. If this were so, would you and Miss Bristol be kind enough to give me your educated assessment of the unknown artifact? My father seemed to think it might prove to be quite valuable, but I am uncertain whether or not I should sell it."

Miss Bristol glanced at Arthur. It was quite obvious which artifact George was referring to.

Arthur said, "I should be more than happy to examine it, but we must choose an appropriate time and place to do so."

Miss Bristol added, "I would also like to see the artifact, Professor Wexley."

"Wonderful, perhaps at lunch tomorrow? I know a lovely restaurant within walking distance, the perfect spot for a quiet discussion. Shall I stop by at noon?"

"Excellent. I am already looking forward to it."

After George had left, Arthur said, "Would you come to my office, please, Miss Bristol? Dr. Boas had a question about one of the maps you drew of the dig in Teotihuacan."

"Of course, Professor."

They walked into Arthur's office, stepping over to a long wooden table, Arthur pointing to one of her carefully drawn maps. He leaned over, his voice low.

"George wants to sell the object, I am certain of it."

"He was questioning the value of it, asking us if he should sell it."

"Quite so, Miss Bristol."

"What shall we do if he will not listen to reason?"

"I do not know. It would seem fate has placed us in another impossible situation."

"George has the objects in his possession?"

"He does."

"That does complicate matters."

"It is a Gordian knot of epic proportions. He will not readily give them up, and more than likely he has them securely hidden away."

Miss Bristol thought for a moment, then said, "Perhaps we could offer to buy the objects back from him.

Is that not his intended goal, to sell them for a profit?"

"An excellent thought, although I have no idea what the cost might be. I have a sizable inheritance left to me by my father, but I doubt it would be enough to satisfy him. A government could offer him far more than I would ever be able to."

"It might be enough, considering that he would be gaining financially, while also doing what he knows in his heart to be the right thing."

Arthur turned to Miss Bristol. "You are a wonder, Miss Bristol. Your plan might very well work. You may have saved the day."

"We shall find out tomorrow."

"So we shall, Miss Bristol."

George arrived promptly at noon the following day, greeting Arthur and Miss Bristol as they stood in Arthur's office.

"Good afternoon. You have not forgotten our luncheon date, I hope? It is a short ten minute walk."

"We have not forgotten."

Arthur and Miss Bristol put their coats on, following George out of Schermerhorn Hall, strolling along 116th Street, Miss Bristol commenting on the lovely weather.

Arthur said, "You have brought the artifact given to you by your father?"

"I did not bring it with me today, but I can describe it in great detail, if that would help."

"Did your father mention what he thought the value of this object might be?"

George pointed down the street. "There is the restaurant, an excellent spot for quiet conversation."

They were soon seated at a secluded table in the corner of the restaurant, the waiter having taken their orders.

George said, "I have no idea the value of the object, but it must be something quite extraordinary, something which would most certainly allow me to buy a stately home of my choice, to marry and raise a family."

Arthur nodded. "As you well know, I fear what would happen if the artifact fell into the wrong hands, and the catastrophic consequences which would surely follow."

"I am well aware of this, but I am also well aware of the vast sum of money such a sale would provide."

"I may have a solution. I would like to buy the object from you. I would offer you fifteen thousand dollars, more than enough to buy a stately home in the city where you could raise a family of your own."

George looked at Arthur curiously. "How do you come to have such a large amount of money?"

"It was left to me by my father. I am offering you the full amount of my inheritance."

"And you would destroy the artifact?"

"I would. I wish we had never found them. I wish I had never looked in the crate of artifacts left by Frederick Beaumont."

Miss Bristol added, "You would gain an impressive home, while taking comfort in the knowledge that you made a noble decision. Professor Hollingsworth's fears about the artifact are well founded. It could bring about an apocalyptic loss of life across the world, entire populations vanishing."

"Somewhat dramatic, Miss Bristol, but I suppose you do make a good point. The world is filled with people like Mr. Crowder who would not hesitate for a moment to use the artifact for their gain."

Arthur said. "What do you think? Do you find my offer satisfactory?"

George shrugged. "I suppose I do. For the princely sum of fifteen thousand dollars, the artifact is yours."

"I thank you, sir. You have made a decision you will not regret."

"I hope so. I shall start my search for a proper home this very day. I have grown weary of our old home."

"It will take me several days to have a check drawn

up for you. You are currently living in Brooklyn?"

"Yes, I am living with my parents. They are not wealthy and never have been. They inherited the home but have only a small monthly income, quite dependent on my salary to provide for their needs. It will take me a day to retrieve the artifact. Perhaps we could meet at this address in two days?" George pulled a piece of paper from his pocket, writing an address on it.

"This is where you are living?"

"It is several blocks away from my home. I do not wish my parents to be aware of this particular transaction."

"I understand. My lips are sealed."

As Arthur and Miss Bristol were returning to Schermerhorn Hall, Arthur said, "You have done it, Miss Bristol, your idea has saved the day. You saved our lives in Teotihuacan, and you have saved the lives of countless millions of people."

"You are the one who sacrificed his inheritance—a far greater sacrifice than any I have made."

"It is only money, it does not bring true happiness, only temporary earthly comforts which often become tiresome."

"And what does bring true happiness? I should like to know your thoughts on this."

"I suppose it would be friendship, family, the ability to find great joy in simple things, to have an eternal sense of wonder about the world we live in."

"Your words never cease to bring me great cheer, Arthur."

"You called me Arthur."

"I did. I must confess that you have become a dear friend."

"May I ask you a personal question, Miss Bristol? If you choose not to answer it, I shall completely understand."

"You may ask your question."

"You will be receiving your honorary degree at the end of the semester, at which time I shall no longer be your mentor. With your honorary degree in hand, you would readily be accepted by Barnard College as an assistant professor of anthropology, if that is your wish. When that time comes, would you allow me the honor of calling on you?"

Miss Bristol smiled. "You already know my answer, Arthur, but when that time comes, I hope you will ask me again."

"I shall indeed, Miss Bristol."

Two days later Arthur stood at the 116th Street subway, waiting for Miss Bristol, giving a quizzical look when he saw her approaching him, dressed in a pale blue fitted jacket with navy velvet lapels, a crisp white blouse with a high laced collar, and a long gored skirt almost concealing her polished buttoned boots, a small embroidered travel bag in one hand, a folded newspaper in her other hand.

"Are you going on trip, Miss Bristol?"

"A short one, I am visiting my grandmother in Yonkers for two days. She does not agree with the new styles, preferring that I wear more ladylike clothes, and so I oblige her when I visit."

"That is most considerate of you, Miss Bristol."

They boarded the subway, arriving at the elevated train platform, taking the train across the East River to Brooklyn. The two friends stepped off the train, Arthur checking the address that George had given them. "It's about a fifteen minute walk."

"Have you spoken to George since he agreed to sell the artifact?"

"I have not. I hope he has not had a change of heart."

"As do I. You are giving him an enormous sum of money, so I can't imagine him turning it down."

"I hope you are right."

"You said Dr. Boas mentioned something about a possible future expedition?"

"He was somewhat guarded, but said it would not

be a return to Teotihuacan. He said the political climate in Mexico is too dangerous at this time because of the impending revolution. He did mention a possible ocean crossing."

"To where? Did he say which ocean?"

"He did not share that with me. He holds his cards close to his chest."

Miss Bristol pointed down the street. "There's George!"

"He's carrying a box. That is a good sign."

"It is indeed."

Arthur tapped his coat. "I have his check in my pocket."

George waved to them as they approached.

Arthur said, "I see you have brought the artifact left to you by your father?"

"I have. And you have brought the check left to you by your father?"

Arthur laughed. "I have."

George motioned them toward an alleyway. "Perhaps a slightly more secluded spot would be appropriate, so you might examine the artifact away from prying eyes."

They stepped down the alleyway, George stopping, flipping the lid of the box open, revealing the weapon they had found in Beaumont's tunnel, two crystalline boxes of charger cylinders sitting next to it.

"It all appears to be in good order." Arthur pulled the check from his pocket. "Your check for fifteen thousand dollars, sir."

George studied the check, then hesitated, his hands gripping the box tightly.

Arthur said, "The check is good, if that is your fear. It is more than enough to buy a fine home."

"I'm sure it is."

"You have concerns over the sale?"

"I have changed my mind this very moment. The artifact is no longer for sale. I can't allow myself to sell it to you."

"But you said you would, you agreed to the price."

"And now I have changed my mind, as is my right."

"Why?"

"Because I realized I want more, a great deal more. I am tired of scrabbling about on the meager salary of a lowly physics professor. I want more than just a stately house; I want a mansion on Fifth Avenue. I want an automobile and a sailing yacht. I want to take cruises to Europe, returning with crates of precious antiques to fill my grand home. I want to dine at the finest restaurants, chatting with the Rockefellers, with J. P. Morgan, with Andrew Carnegie. That is what I want, and that is why I shall be selling the artifact to the military."

A dark frown appeared on Miss Bristol's face. "You would enjoy a pleasant day of sailing in your yacht, while millions of people across the world perish; men, women, and children crying out in terror as they lose their lives inside the green bubbles? Your money would bring you warm comfort as you dined on lobster in a fine restaurant with your wealthy friends, ignoring the plight of the world?"

Anger rippled across George's face. "Such noble and self-righteous words from a woman who has everything. You could have any man you want—marry a Rockefeller, live in luxury for the rest of your days. You know nothing of my plight, Miss Bristol, being trapped in an old house with my aging parents."

Arthur intervened. "Please, George, let us think calmly about this. I'm sure we can reach a mutually satisfactory solution. I can raise more money, if that would help."

"Can you raise ten million dollars? That seems like an appropriate sum for a weapon such as this."

"You know that is quite impossible. Please, think about how this would affect the world, all the lives lost."

"To be quite candid, I do not care how it would

affect the world; I only care about how it shall affect me."

"You can't sell it; I won't allow such a thing to happen."

George laughed. "You won't allow it? You and Miss Bristol really have no idea how the real world works, sitting in your safe little offices studying long-forgotten civilizations that no one cares about."

Arthur's jaw tightened. "You are not going to sell the weapon, George."

George gave a derisive laugh. "Is Miss Bristol going to murder me, as she murdered Mr. Crowder? I didn't hear you complaining about Crowder dying, so why begin now?"

George pulled the weapon from the box, pressing the tab on the grip, the barrel glowing with a pulsating green light, a low humming sound filling the alleyway. "Would you care to borrow this for a moment, Miss Bristol, so you can put an end to me, you and Arthur living happily ever after? You think I don't know about you two? It is quite obvious, I assure you."

Arthur glared at George. "You have gone too far, sir. Give me the weapon."

"And if I don't?"

Arthur took a step forward, George aiming the

weapon at him. “One more step and you shall be joining Mr. Crowder in the great beyond.”

“You won’t shoot me. That is not the man you are, George.” He stepped forward again, reaching out for the gun.

George pressed the firing tab on the weapon, the brilliant beam of white light hitting Arthur, the green bubble surrounding him.

Arthur turned, his eyes on Miss Bristol, his lips moving, saying something she could not hear. There was a brilliant flash of light and he was gone, a horrifying cry of anguish erupting from Miss Bristol.

“You killed him! You killed Arthur! You killed him!”

“It was not my fault, he was coming for me. I had no choice, just as you had no choice when you killed Crowder.”

An eerie calmness filled Miss Bristol, her voice low and deliberate. “I will tell everyone what you have done. I will tell the police. I will tell the university. I will tell your parents. You will never—”

“You will tell no one, Miss Bristol.”

George aimed the weapon at Miss Bristol, pressing the firing tab.

Chapter 19

We meet ourselves time and again in a thousand disguises on the path of life. —Carl Jung

Miss Bristol

Miss Bristol stood up, her eyes on the sepia tone photograph of her, Arthur, and George standing in front of The Temple of the Feathered Serpent. She remembered it now as if it was yesterday—Arthur had handed his folding camera to Mr. Crowder, asking him to take their picture. Arthur and George had given her the honor of holding up the first artifact they found, the small greenstone figurine in her hand. It was one of the happiest moments of her life.

She touched the image of Arthur, her heart aching. Dear Arthur was gone. He was truly gone from her life. They were all gone; everyone she had known, everyone she had ever loved was gone.

She turned the pages of the photo album, studying the photos one after another, dozens of them, images of their expedition to Teotihuacan: standing on the promenade of the *SS Merida*, Arthur standing next to her. She had been so excited, so happy. There were pictures of New York Harbor, of the elegant hotel in Veracruz, the three of them dressed in their finest clothes in the dining room, smiling, the expedition still ahead of them.

She carefully removed a photograph of her and Arthur standing in front of the Pyramid of the Sun, both of them holding shovels, both of them smiling. He had laughingly said it would be a good photo to show Dr. Boas. She slipped it into her pocket, pressing her hand against it. She would treasure it for the rest of her days. As she was closing the album she noted the inscription inside the front cover.

Property of Professor George Wexley
1910 Expedition to Teotihuacan

She could not bear to see his name, closing the album. She turned, studying the glass case of artifacts. After everything that had happened, why would George have these artifacts? He was a professor of physics, not anthropology. Where did he get them, and why did he want them? Surely not to remember the events that took place during the expedition, and most certainly not the events which had occurred after their return to New York.

Miss Bristol clearly understood the purpose of the otherworldly artifact now. It was not a death ray, as they had thought. The device didn't kill, it sent its target into the future, temporarily erasing their memories. The visitors did not wish to kill living creatures, but on occasion it must have been necessary for them to remove a threat, or perhaps to remove themselves from a life threatening situation. They must have visited thousands of other worlds, facing innumerable frightening creatures of all shapes and sizes.

She grabbed the photo albums when she heard the front door open, quickly placing them back in the glass case, locking it, hanging the key on the nail.

"Miss Bristol?"

Miss Bristol picked up a feather duster, calling out, "I'm upstairs, Mrs. Smith, doing some cleaning."

She heard footsteps come slowly up the stairs, Mrs. Smith stepping into the room, Miss Bristol dusting the roll top desk.

"Thank you, dear. Father's room does seem to gather dust."

"Mrs. Smith, I noticed an envelope on the desk

addressed to Professor George Wexley. Was he your father?"

"He was indeed, Miss Bristol, and I miss him every day."

"I have been reading a number of books on anthropology which I have found to be quite fascinating. Your father was an anthropologist?"

"No, he was a professor of physics at Columbia University."

"How interesting. How long was he a professor there?"

"Most of his life. He retired at age seventy-one as head of the physics department. He was quite brilliant."

Miss Bristol tried to make sense of this new information. Had George not sold the weapon to the military?

"I'm curious as to why he would have a glass case filled with ancient artifacts if he was a physics professor?"

"He went on an expedition to Teotihuacan, Mexico in 1910, and apparently it was quite a memorable time for him. He used to say he had never been happier than he was during those three months. He would often take out the photo album and look at it, slowly turning the pages. I don't know why the expedition affected him so much, but it did. Perhaps because archeology was so different from physics, a welcome break from his work at the university. It became a hobby for him, collecting artifacts, studying them. In the end, he was quite knowledgable about such things."

"He must have been a wonderful father."

"He changed over the years, as we all do, becoming more empathetic, a kinder soul, as he grew older. I believe he suffered from deep depression at times, mostly in his later years, but he fought it, always trying to remain cheerful."

"You said he vanished?"

"He did. I came home from work one day and he was gone. There was no note, no explanation. Sometimes I wonder if he lost his battle against depression, perhaps took his own life."

"I'm sorry, it was not my intention to pry."

"That's all right, dear. It is the nature of this world, and we must look it in the eye and learn from it. That's what he would always say to me."

Miss Bristol was baffled. The man Mrs. Smith was describing sounded nothing like the man who had shot her and Arthur with the ancient weapon. A thought occurred to her, remembering that Mrs. Smith said her father had vanished. Had he used the time gun on himself? Sent himself into the future, perhaps hoping for a new and better world, beginning again as a young man?

As she was gazing across the room, her eyes stopped on a wooden box sitting on top of a bookcase. She was certain it was the wooden box George had been carrying when he met them in the alleyway. Was the time gun still in it?

"Was this the house where your father grew up?"

"It was, dear. It has been in the family for four generations. I will be the last, since Albert and I never had children. The world has changed; people move around so much these days, no one stays put anymore. Houses like this belong to a different time, a different world. How about we go downstairs and have a nice lunch?"

"That sounds wonderful. I'd love to hear more about what it was like growing up here. Did your father collect antiques? My father used to collect antique guns. He said they all had an interesting history."

"I suppose he did collect quite a few antiques. As far as guns, I know he had several old revolvers, and I remember finding an odd looking gun in a wooden box as a child, when I was poking around in his office. I asked him about it, and he said it was a toy ray gun from his childhood. We do cherish our old toys, don't we? Those are such impressionable years."

Miss Bristol nodded. "They are."

"Miss Bristol, may I ask you a personal question?"

"Of course."

"You seem like an exceptionally perceptive young woman, someone who could be doing much more with her life than cleaning houses. Have you any thoughts of furthering your education?"

Miss Bristol thought for a moment, then said, "I have felt lost for some time, uncertain what to do with my life, but I think those days are over. I am quite certain now that attending a university will be in my future, but it is not something I can afford at this time. When I do attend university, I should like to study anthropology."

"That's wonderful, I am so pleased to hear that. You know, Columbia University has a fine anthropology department, and I still know quite a number of people there. I could write you a letter of recommendation. Of course, Father's friends in the anthropology department are long gone, but he was well known and highly respected there. A letter from me would carry a certain amount of weight. You said you can't afford the tuition now, but I would like to help you with that, if you would let me. Father left everything he had to me, a substantial inheritance. He made wise investments over the years and did quite well for himself. I have no one to leave my money to, so I may as well spend it on something worthwhile while I am still here. Father always stressed the need for education—he would be more than pleased to hear that his money was going toward your degree in anthropology."

Miss Bristol desperately wished Arthur was here to see this. Fate did indeed have a curious sense of humor—George would be paying for her degree in anthropology.

"What do you say, Miss Bristol?"

"It's such a large sum of money, and you scarcely know me."

"I am an excellent judge of character, and for some curious reason, I feel as if I do know you, as if we were old friends. Life is like that sometimes—you meet someone and just hit it off from day one."

Miss Bristol could not deny that fate had once again intervened in her life, opening a door for her. "In that case, I most gratefully accept your offer, Mrs. Smith. I will work hard and do well, I can promise you that."

"I know you will. Father would have liked you. I sometimes think if he had it to do over, he would have liked a career in anthropology instead of physics."

Miss Bristol headed home after finishing her cleaning, Mrs. Smith saying she would write a letter of recommendation, and when Miss Bristol was ready, she would make several phone calls to people she knew at Columbia.

Miss Bristol had no idea what she would write in her application to the university regarding her background and previous education, but finally decided she would tell them a version of the truth—that she had amnesia and had no idea who she was or where she came from. Despite their thorough search, the police were unable to discover who she was. She would tell the university she was starting over, a clean slate, making the best of a difficult situation; something which was quite true. She imagined the looks on their faces if she told them she had been months away from receiving an honorary anthropology degree back in 1910. She also knew that even with her current knowledge of anthropology, she needed to go back to school, that a great many significant discoveries had been made since 1910. Silas had recently told her that scientists today can see what is under the ground without ever digging up the earth, using some sort of scanning device to search for ancient buried ruins or hidden tunnels. She would have loved to have had a device like that during their expedition in Teotihuacan.

She stopped short when she approached her house, staring at it with new eyes, with new memories. It was like meeting a dear old friend out of the blue, someone you haven't seen in years. She was looking at the house where she had grown up. She knew every room in it now, every nook and cranny. She used to play in the room she was renting. It had been at times her castle, a pirate cove, a treasure room, a wizard's lair. That was why the house and the room had felt so comforting, why it felt like home.

As she gazed at the house, she desperately wished there was someone she could share her memories with, but it was not to be. She was alone in this new world.

She darted up the stairs, entering the house, Mrs. Wiggins calling out, "Dinner in half an hour, Miss Bristol. Don't forget to wash your hands."

"I won't forget." She ran up the stairs to her room, stopping outside her door, staring down the hallway at the wooden folding ladder that led up to the attic. She had climbed it many times as a child, exploring the attic. She had to be certain that all this was true, that the artifact was still there. She ran over to the ladder, pulling it down, climbing up into the attic, clicking on an overhead light. If it was there, it would be back in the far corner, hidden amongst the eaves.

She made her way past the old boxes and suitcases and dusty furniture to the far side of the attic, stopping when she saw the oak bookshelf sitting against the wall. She stepped over to it, kneeling down, running her hand across the books, the set of encyclopedias her father had given her when she was ten years old.

She sat silently, remembering how thrilled she had been when he presented the books to her. The first thing she looked up was the pyramids of Egypt, hoping to discover how they had been built. The gift of encyclopedias was such a kindness on her father's part, and she hoped he knew how much it had meant to her.

She stepped over to the corner of the attic, reaching tentatively down into the eves, giving a sigh of relief when her fingers touched a cloth bag. It was still here. She retrieved the bag, loosening the drawstring, taking out the time gun, cradling it in her hands. She wished with all her heart they had never found it. She would have spent a lifetime with Arthur, perhaps had children, raised a family together. She hesitated, then pressed the tab on the back of the grip, the barrel glowing with a pale green light, a humming sound filling the air. It still worked.

She stared at the gun, knowing she could leave this world right now for another one, leave all this behind her, but what would she have to gain from that? And what about the people she left behind? How would her disappearance affect Mrs. Wiggins and Harlan, after already losing their daughter Anna? How would it affect Silas, a boy still trying to cope with the tragic loss of his sister?

She tapped the button again, the humming sound stopping, placing the artifact back in the bag with the silver charging cylinders, returning it to its hiding place in the eaves. Finding the artifact and the encyclopedias was the final proof she needed. All her memories were real, all the events of 1910 had happened.

She headed back down to the kitchen after washing her hands, helping Mrs. Wiggins prepare dinner, watching Silas do his homework, listening to his jokes, laughing at them. It was curious how a small thing like Mrs. Wiggins reminding her to wash her hands could bring her such comfort. It felt like home.

Harlan stepped through the front door ten minutes later, walking down the hallway, entering the kitchen. "Something smells good."

"Miss Bristol has been helping me prepare dinner."

"Wonderful. Sorry I'm late, I'm on a new case, a big one."

Silas looked up. "Is it a gruesome murder?"

Mrs. Wiggins frowned. “Silas, please.”

Harlan said, “My lips are sealed, but yes, it’s a murder, a high profile one. It will be front page news tomorrow, all over the internet.”

Miss Bristol gave a wry smile. It was 2025, but it might well have been 1910. The world had changed, technology had changed, but people had not.

Harlan took a seat at the table, his eyes on Silas. “Tell me one thing you learned in school today.”

“Don’t tell a girl she throws like a girl?”

He laughed. “A valuable lesson indeed. And what was the price you paid to learn this?”

Silas pulled up his sleeve, revealing a bruise on his arm.

Harlan laughed again. “A small price to pay for such a valuable life lesson.”

“I apologized and so did she.”

“Even better. Are you friends now?”

“Um, she’s my girlfriend?”

Mrs. Wiggins spun around. “You have a girlfriend? You are not old enough to have a girl friend.”

“If you think about it logically, I do have a girlfriend, so therefore, I must be old enough to have one.” He grinned.

Miss Bristol stifled a laugh. This was wonderful, this was life.

Four days later, Miss Bristol arrived at Mrs. Smith's house, finding a note on the kitchen table saying she would not be home until late afternoon, that she was visiting a friend. Miss Bristol headed directly upstairs to George's office, anxious to examine the box which had once held the time gun.

She had initially felt some guilt about unlocking the glass cabinet and looking through the photo albums, but when she had asked Mrs. Smith about the photographs a few days later, after her memories had returned, Mrs. Smith gladly took the albums out to show her the photos, the two of them sitting down together, Mrs. Smith slowly turning the pages. She said it was fun to look through old photos with someone else, but not to look at them by herself, remembering days gone by, remembering all the people who were gone now.

Miss Bristol carried a wooden chair over to the bookcase, stepping up onto it and retrieving the wooden box. She hopped off the chair, setting the box on a table, raising the lid of the box. The gun was gone, but there was an envelope sitting in the box. Curious about its contents, Miss Bristol reached in and retrieved it. She turned the envelope over, almost dropping it when she saw the handwriting on it.

MISS BRISTOL RENTS A ROOM

For Arthur and Miss Bristol

Her hands were shaking as she opened the envelope, unfolding the letter, reading it.

Chapter 20

Dear Arthur and Miss Bristol,

I am writing this because my days here are coming to an end, and there are things I wish you to know. Should one or both of you be reading this, then you already know what the artifact does. What you will not know is the depth of my regret for the events that took place in that alleyway so many years ago. I live with it every day—I still see your faces. You were friends, and I betrayed your trust. I have never forgiven myself for what I did, and I never will. I am not even sure God will forgive me, although I hope that shall not be the case. I was wrong, I was a fool. I was misguided by avarice, looking outside myself for something that I now know can only be found within us. It has taken me many years, most of my life, to understand what I believe both of you already knew; that happiness, contentment, and acceptance of ourselves comes from within us, not from wealth or fame or our standing in society. I can't undo what has been done, but I can tell you I am profoundly sorry for what I did, and every day I seek redemption by my actions. I did marry, and we had a lovely daughter, Clara, raising her in the family home. She knows nothing of what happened, nor is she aware of the artifacts we found.

As you know, the artifact was not a terrifying death ray, but something else entirely, a weapon that does not kill, but does successfully remove a threat. I never sold the gun to the military. It had been my intention to do so, but I attempted to first discover everything I could about the weapon before I sold it, something I felt to be a good negotiation tactic. However, the more I came to understand its purpose and function, the less determined I became to sell it. The day arrived when I put it back in the box and set it on top of the bookshelf. You were both right about humanity not being ready for such a device as this.

During my experimentation with the weapon I came to realize it sent living creatures into the future, that realization coming only after discovering the cylindrical knob beneath the barrel. When I pressed it in and turned it all the way counterclockwise, then fired it at an insect, the insect vanished, but then, much to my astonishment, it reappeared in a flash of white light a short time later. I suspect that the gun uses random projection times unless the control knob is used to select specific ones. In other words, we can project someone to a somewhat specific time in the future. I have no idea what the maximum projection time is, or how the artifact works. Even as the head of the physics department, I am completely baffled by the science behind the device. I can tell you that each silver charging cylinder provides for fifteen shots of the gun.

I should tell you both that when questioned about your disappearance by the university officials and the police, I told them I suspected you had run away together, that you had fallen in love, that you knew a public relationship between a professor and a research assistant would be scandalous, bringing shame to the university and spelling an end to both of your careers. I suggested that you may have both moved to Mexico. They had no reason to think otherwise, and the matter was quickly dropped. It was certainly not an event the university wished to publicize. Mrs. Fletcher told me in confidence that Dr. Boas had been furious when he heard you had run off together, saying he would make certain your names would never again be associated with Columbia University.

Imagine my surprise when I saw Arthur walking past my house in 1968. I recognized him instantly as Arthur, or a younger version of him. Arthur, when Clara hired you as a gardener, you had not recovered your memories. To be quite honest, although I recognized you, I was afraid to talk to you, afraid you might remember who I was and what I had done. I felt such shame.

I am quite ill now, something I have kept hidden from Clara. As you may or may not know, the body you arrive in is not the one you left with, but it is genetically identical, and does hold all your memories, although it takes an uncertain amount of time for them to be restored. You arrive young and healthy. That being said, I will tell you that I am going to use the artifact to project myself forward, my closest guess is somewhere around 2080, bringing with me a letter explaining who I am, where I am from and how the artifact works. I am looking forward to seeing the scientific advances we have made by then, if we haven't already destroyed ourselves and our planet.

My leaving will sadden my daughter, but in some ways it will be easier for her, considering the impending unpleasantness of my illness. I should like to add, if you decide to move forward in time using your artifact, I would be more than pleased to see both of you again in 2080. I should mention one further discovery I made regarding the artifact: if the two of you stand close together when the gun is fired, both of you will be projected to the same point in time.

With deepest apologies,
George

Miss Bristol was stunned, reading the letter three times. She finally folded it up, placing it in her pocket. Her feelings were deeply conflicted regarding George's apology. His craving for wealth and social status had taken Arthur away from her, undoubtedly the most searingly painful moment of her life. For that, she was not certain that she could ever forgive him. On the other hand, he seemed to have sincerely changed his ways, coming to understand that his own sense of worth, his value as a person, must come from within, not from such things as wealth and social standing, or dining on lobster with the Rockefellers. Arthur had once told her that seeking great wealth was like eating ravenously in a dream when you are hungry—it provides no nourishment and does nothing to assuage your true hunger.

Miss Bristol returned the box to its place on the bookshelf, then took a seat in a leather armchair, leaning back, her thoughts returning to George. He had learned an important lesson in his life, but he had made unforgivable choices along the way. Perhaps the purpose of life is to learn such difficult lessons. She knew her lessons were not the same as George's, and not the same as Arthur's. Perhaps dear Arthur had been right, perhaps her lesson was to learn forgiveness—to forgive herself for the death of Mr. Crowder, and to forgive others, like George. She knew this lesson would prove to be as difficult for her as George's lesson had been for him.

If there was a reason for everything, as Arthur had said, why had he been taken away from her, the love of her life, and why had she been sent by fate to be alone in a new and unfamiliar world?

She had no answers to these questions, but here she was, sitting in George's office in the year 2025. She tried to imagine what Arthur would say to her. More than likely, he would tell her she should press on, no matter what obstacles fate had set before her. Whatever the reason was for her presence here, she should make the best of it. That was what Arthur might say, and it was something she agreed with. They were of one mind on this.

The next evening at dinner, Miss Bristol said, "I have some wonderful news. Mrs. Smith has said she would like to pay for my tuition at Columbia University, if I were to be accepted as a student there."

Mrs. Wiggins said, "That is wonderful news, Miss Bristol. Are you going to apply?"

Harlan said, "Not to rain on your parade, Miss Bristol, but Columbia won't accept you without proper identification."

Mrs. Wiggins frowned. "There must be something we can do. Can't we just tell them she has amnesia?"

"There is something I can do, but it will take months. As a member of law enforcement, I can file an appeal with the courts to give her a new legal identity. I've done it several times before. If all goes well, they will issue you a social security number and a New York City identification card. You'll be good to go."

Miss Bristol had no idea what a social security number was, but made a mental note to research it on her phone. "Would I then be able to attend university?"

"It should be no problem if you are accepted, but it will take five or six months, maybe longer, to jump through all the bureaucratic hoops."

Mrs. Wiggins said, "You'll have to wait until the

fall semester to apply, almost a year from now."

"That will give me time to prepare, to study. There are a great many things I have forgotten that I should like to read about." Miss Bristol had no idea what events had transpired between 1910 and 2025, but if she attended university she would need to have a thorough knowledge of those events.

Miss Bristol settled into a routine, working three days a week at Mrs. Smith's home, while spending the rest of the week reading about world events that occurred since 1910, both cultural and scientific, something which she found to be quite fascinating.

Harlan surprised her when he came home one evening with a desktop computer for her, saying it was not good for her eyes to be reading so much on her smartphone. Silas was more than happy to show her how it worked, and how to play games on it.

It was a brisk Monday morning that found Miss Bristol strolling along Moore Street, running a few errands for Mrs. Smith. She was looking at her phone as she walked, laughing at a funny image Silas had texted to her. He had used an app to give himself an enormous beard and a pirate hat. He felt like a younger brother now, something she had never had growing up, being the only child.

She looked up from her phone, spotting Mama

Rosa's Pizza across the street, checking the time. It was almost lunchtime. Perhaps Ben would be there. It would be lovely to see him. She could show off her new phone, tell him she knew all about the internet now, including how credit cards work. She would show him the debit card that Mrs. Wiggins had gotten her so she wouldn't have to carry cash around. However, as much as she liked Ben, she would not tell him her memories had returned. To tell anyone about her memories would undoubtedly have disastrous consequences.

She crossed the street, scanning the tables, but Ben was nowhere to be seen. She stepped inside, ordering two slices of pepperoni pizza, making a joke with the clerk, laughing at his reply. She headed outside, pizza in hand, taking a seat at an empty table. She was reading about the events leading up to World War II on her phone when she was interrupted by a familiar voice.

"Miss Bristol, it is a pleasure to see you again. Might I join you?"

She looked up, smiling brightly when she saw Ben standing at her table. "Of course, that would be wonderful. It is so nice to see you. I have an extra slice of pizza if you would like."

"I would indeed like that, thank you so much." He reached into his coat pocket, pulling out his wallet.

Miss Bristol held up her hand. "No, this is my treat, I insist. You have helped me far more than you can ever know."

"You are too kind, Miss Bristol."

Miss Bristol stopped short, an image of the Pyramid of the Sun flashing through her thoughts. She slowly lowered the pizza, turning to Ben, studying his eyes, the light of recognition blinking on.

"Arthur."

He smiled at her, nodding. "Your memories have finally returned."

She could not take her eyes off him. "They have. Is it really you? It feels like a dream to me."

"It is not a dream, although this moment does indeed feel like one. We are of one mind on that, Miss Bristol."

"Why didn't you tell me who you were? When you first saw me, you could have said something, told me who I was, where I came from."

"Imagine this, if you would, Miss Bristol: you are having lunch at a restaurant, a delicious slice of pepperoni pizza, when an old man approaches you, a man you have never seen before. The man insists that you are a time traveler from the year 1910, transported here by an ancient alien artifact. What would your response be?"

Miss Bristol laughed. “An excellent point, dear Arthur. You are forgiven.”

“You called me dear Arthur.”

“In my secret thoughts I have always called you dear Arthur. Tell me everything, by what miracle you came to be here on the same day I arrived.”

“It was both a miracle and not a miracle. I arrived in the same fashion as you, I imagine, with a terrible headache and dreadful nausea, but I landed in the year 1968. I was taken to Bellevue Hospital by ambulance, having cut my face when I fainted after arriving, having no memory of who I was or where I came from. The doctors at Bellevue examined me, but could find no physical reasons for my amnesia, suspecting I had experienced some sort of traumatic event which caused my memory loss.”

“They said the same of me, but I could not remember any such event.”

“Neither could I. They placed me in a group home, where people who needed assistance and guidance lived. I made a friend there, a man named Sky who had been a psychology student at Columbia, dropping out for personal reasons. He called me King Arthur because I could only remember my first name. I had a name now, I knew who I was. I was King Arthur exploring a new world.

"We became friends, exploring the city together. I learned a great deal from him about this new world: what clothes to wear, how to buy things, how to navigate the subway system, how to take a bus, how to make phone calls, but most importantly, how to freely voice the myriad of thoughts and feelings I kept prisoner inside of me. I could not recall my memories, but felt strangely guided by them, led unerringly to the spot where I had hidden a bag of gold coins given to me by my grandparents when I became a professor at Columbia."

Miss Bristol laughed. "How curious, I also had gold coins in my travel bag, coins which were meant for my grandmother, a gift from my parents. I sold a single twenty dollar gold coin for over three thousand dollars. I was stunned."

Arthur laughed. "If you remember correctly, I believe I was the one who sold the coin for you?"

"Of course you were, I wasn't thinking."

"I was as stunned as you when I sold several of my gold coins. It wasn't until I visited the Museum of Natural History that my knowledge of anthropology unexpectedly returned, something which led to a position there as a research assistant. Despite the return of those memories, I still had no idea who I was or where I came from."

"When did the rest of your memories return, memories of us, of Teotihuacan?"

"I often had dreams of a girl with orange hair, but did not know her name, only that she was a dear and cherished friend. Three long years passed before I remembered who you were, who I was. I was walking past a construction site and saw a man wearing khaki clothing, digging with a long handled shovel in the rocky soil. When I heard the sound of the steel shovel scraping against rocks and earth, my thoughts returned to Teotihuacan and I remembered everything.

"I realized that George would have been forced to use the artifact on you, since you had been a witness to what he had done. I suspected you would arrive in the same spot as I had, in the alleyway, but I had no idea when that would be, whether it would be before or after I arrived. I stayed in this area, always looking for you, the girl with the orange hair. And then, after so many years, there you were, sitting at this table, just as I remembered you. I did not want to startle you, but I wanted to help you remember."

"Why did you use the name Ben?"

"My middle name is Benjamin. When I was growing up everyone called me Ben. I thought it would be best if you remembered my name on your own."

Chapter 21

Miss Bristol said, “You knew the room I rented was in my family home?”

“I did. I walked past your house on a number of occasions over the years, thinking perhaps you had been guided there by your memories. It was a curious coincidence that the Room-for-Rent sign had been placed in the window on the day of your arrival.”

“I should think it was far more than a curious coincidence. I have come to think of the Wiggins as a second family. They have been so kind to me, almost treating me as a daughter. Their own daughter tragically passed a year ago.”

“I am sorry to hear that. The loss of a child is unbearable. I’m glad they have treated you with such kindness. I have found most people to be more than kind, offering help and guidance if they were able.”

“There is something I need to tell you.”

“What is it?”

“I know what happened to George. I know

everything. I was hired by a woman named Mrs. Smith to be her housekeeper. It is beyond astonishing, but the woman turned out to be George's daughter, Clara Smith. I could not believe it was so."

"That is startling indeed, even more so because I had an almost identical experience. I did not realize it until after my memories had returned, but I was also hired by Clara Smith, as a gardener."

"That is astonishing. Was George still there? Clara said he disappeared in 1972."

"He was there, I saw him. I was sitting on the front porch with Clara, when her father came out to meet me. I had not the slightest idea her father was George, but I had a strange feeling about him, the way he looked at me. When he set a small stone figurine on the table in front of me, a single word came out of my mouth—Tláloc, the name of the deity. I had no idea what the word meant, but he picked up the figurine and put his hand on my shoulder, saying, 'I hope your memory returns, young man. I am truly sorry'. He must have known who I was, and he said he was sorry. My friend Sky said such powerful events as these are not coincidences at all. He said they are called synchronistic events and hold deep meaning. He said we are guided by unseen forces, but those forces come from within us."

"I would agree with your friend Sky. It was no accident that I was hired by George's daughter to be her housekeeper. I was in George's office when my memories returned. I was looking through an old photo album and came across the photograph of you, me, and George standing in front of The Temple of the Feathered Serpent. I remembered everything, the air shimmering around me, surrounded by a pale green mist."

"I was also surrounded by the green mist when my memories returned. It must have something to do with the green bubbles, some kind of residual energy field, perhaps. Do you know what happened to George after we were gone? Did he sell the artifact to the military? I have heard nothing about such a device in my time here, but I suppose it could be a closely guarded military secret."

"He did not sell it." Miss Bristol reached into her purse, pulling out George's letter, handing it to Arthur. "I found this letter in the wooden box that once held George's artifact. It explains everything."

Arthur began to read, his shoulders sagging. "This brings back such powerful memories. I'm glad he didn't sell it."

Finally he put the letter down, handing it to Miss Bristol. She said, "Now that you have read his letter, have your feelings changed about what he did?"

Arthur said, "Over the years I have tried to forgive him, and I think perhaps I have. He knew a great deal about physics, but he had much to learn about himself, about who he was and his purpose in life. What he did in 1910 was the only thing he could have done at that time, being the person he was then. It was all he knew."

Miss Bristol said, "I have not had time to forgive him for taking you away from me, or for taking me away from my parents. I never would have run off and not told them where I was going. It must have hurt them deeply. I can't forgive him for hurting my parents like that."

"I understand."

"He sent himself forward in time to 2080, taking the artifact with him."

"I saw that. Do you have the second artifact? Were you able to locate it?"

"I had hidden it in the attic of my house, the house I now live in. It's still there, and it still works."

"I'm glad it was not lost, not in the hands of people who would use it for their own dark purposes."

"Arthur, may I ask you something of a personal nature? You don't need to answer the question if you don't wish to, but it is something I have always wondered about."

"Anything."

"After George fired the weapon at you, when you were in the green bubble, you turned to me and said something that I could not hear. What did you say?"

Arthur's face softened. "I said I loved you. It was one of the feelings I held captive inside of me for a very long time."

"I was hoping those were your words. I love you, too. I always have."

Arthur reached out, taking Miss Bristol's hand. "Our timing is less than perfect. I am old, you are young."

"All I see is you; all I see is my dear Arthur."

"I have difficult news for you, and a favor to ask of you."

"Anything."

"I am ill, the doctors telling me I should get my affairs in order."

Miss Bristol tried to process Arthur's news. "We have just found each other. It can't be so."

"I would ask you to use the artifact on me, project me into the future, where I shall be young again."

"George said if we stand together we shall be projected forward to the same point in time. We can go together."

"We will both lose our memories again; you will

have forgotten me, and I shall have forgotten you. Who knows what might happen, the world might be far different then, far more dangerous— perhaps we would become separated, lost to each other, the artifact lost. If I go alone, at least I will know you are safe here, your whole life ahead of you, and you will be there to watch over the artifact."

Miss Bristol thought for a minute, then said, "Where do you live? Is it close by?"

"It is. Why do you ask?"

"I want to see your house. I want to see where you live."

"Of course, but what about the artifact?"

"I should like to see your house first."

They left the restaurant together, walking three blocks to Arthur's house, a stately old home that closely resembled George's house.

"This is beautiful, your garden is lovely."

"I have become quite an accomplished gardener over the years, thanks to Clara Smith."

"Do you know your neighbors? Are you on friendly terms with them?"

"That is a curious question, but the answer is yes. We are on excellent terms. You are up to something, Miss Bristol, I can tell. I can almost hear the wheels spinning in your head."

Miss Bristol laughed. "You are perceptive as always."

They headed up the stairs, Arthur opening the front door for her.

Miss Bristol gazed at the interior of the home, feeling as if she had been transported back in time to 1910. "You have kept the house exactly as it was when it was built."

"It would outwardly appear to be so, but I had it completely remodeled and updated a number of years ago."

"It does not look updated."

Arthur called out, "Messages?"

A woman's voice echoed through the entryway. "Good afternoon, Arthur. You have four new texts and twelve emails. Would you like me to read them to you?"

"Not now, thank you."

"You have forgotten to lock the front door and set the alarm. Shall I do that for you?"

"Yes, please."

Miss Bristol heard the front door lock click shut. She gaped at Arthur. "Who is that?"

"It's a computer, artificial intelligence. It controls everything in the house."

"That is astonishing, magical."

"You know as well as I, Miss Bristol, that magic is nothing more than science we don't understand. Come, let us go sit in the living room."

Miss Bristol said, "These paintings are lovely. Were they done by the French impressionists?"

"They were. That one is by Monet, the other, Gaugin."

"The oriental carpet is exquisite." She turned slowly, giving him a curious look. "Arthur, are you wealthy?"

"I made an excellent living as the Curator of Mexican & Central American Archaeology at the American Museum of Natural History."

"You spent a lifetime doing what you love. You once said there is no better way to live your life than that."

"And I sold the sleeve of fabric found by Frederick Beaumont for sixty million dollars."

Miss Bristol burst out laughing. "You did not!"

"I did indeed, Miss Bristol. They said it would take decades to understand how it works, but it would be well worth it. After I go, all this will be yours, everything I have I shall leave to you."

Miss Bristol pointed to the couch. "Sit."

Arthur took a seat, Miss Bristol sitting down next to him, taking his hand. "You once said I was a marvel, that my ideas never ceased to amaze you."

"I remember quite clearly saying that. It is true, I have never met anyone as clever as you."

Miss Bristol smiled. "Then you will not be surprised at all when I tell you I have a plan. But first, there is something you must do."

Four days later, Miss Bristol and Arthur stood on the front steps of his neighbor's house, Arthur knocking on the door, a middle-aged woman answering.

"Arthur, how nice to see you. And who is this lovely young lady?"

"This is my granddaughter, she has been kind enough to come and stay with me for a while. I wanted to let you know that my illness has progressed, and I shall be leaving this afternoon for a hospital in Paris where they are testing an experimental new treatment. While I am gone, my granddaughter will be staying here, taking care of my house for me."

The woman put her hand over her mouth. "Oh, no, I'm so sorry, Arthur. I hope it all works out, that the new treatment works. Is there anything we can do? Anything at all?"

"I shall be fine. I just wanted to introduce my granddaughter to you, so you wouldn't wonder who the strange girl with the orange hair was. Her name is Miss Bristol, something she was called as a child, and it just stuck with her." Arthur laughed.

"It's a pleasure to meet you, Miss Bristol. Please take good care of your grandpa. We all love him dearly—you couldn't ask for a nicer neighbor. He has helped us more times than I can count."

"Thank you, I will."

Arthur and Miss Bristol headed back to Arthur's house, stepping inside. Miss Bristol said, "You called your friends at the museum?"

"I told them the same thing, that my granddaughter was here visiting, that my illness was progressing, and I was going to Paris for a special experimental treatment."

"It must have been difficult for them to hear that."

"It was. The story would be true if we did not have the artifact."

The following morning Miss Bristol arrived at Arthur's house, the computer voice welcoming her as she stepped onto the front porch.

"Good morning, Miss Bristol. Are you here to see Arthur?"

"I am, he is expecting me."

"Splendid, I know he will be pleased to see you, as you are a dear friend of his. Shall I tell him you're here?"

"Yes, please."

A minute later the lock clicked, the door swinging open, Arthur greeting her with a smile.

Miss Bristol stepped inside, the door closing behind her, the lock clicking again.

"I have locked the door and set the alarm, Arthur."

"Thank you."

"How did the computer know it was me at the door?"

"It remembers faces. When you were here before it asked me what your name was, and if we were friends."

"It is all quite astonishing."

"As astonishing as a time gun that sends us to the future?"

"There is nothing more astonishing than that."

"Are we ready?"

"What if something goes wrong?"

"Then we will make the best of it."

Miss Bristol nodded, stepping over to the mahogany table in the entryway, removing the time gun from its cloth bag. "Are you quite certain?"

"I am more than certain. I am ready to begin a new life."

Miss Bristol stepped over to him, putting her arms around him. "I want to hug you forever before you go. We have had the most unlikely of adventures together, you and I, dear Arthur."

"You are the love of my life, Miss Bristol."

"The love of many lives, I hope."

Arthur laughed. "Of course. When we were setting out for Teotihuacan aboard the *SS Merida*, could you have ever imagined such a strange series of events occurring?"

"Not in a thousand years."

Arthur said, "I wonder where Mr. Crowder is now?"

"Perhaps he is in the distant future, aboard one of H.G. Wells' rocket ships bound for Mars."

"A good place for him. He was a dastardly scoundrel, but perhaps he has changed, just as George did."

"Perhaps."

They held each other silently for a long time, Arthur finally stepping away from Miss Bristol. "I am ready, if you are."

Miss Bristol nodded, pressing the tab on the grip of the time gun, the barrel glowing with a pulsating green light.

Arthur smiled. "Until we meet again, Miss Bristol."

"Until we meet again, dear Arthur."

Miss Bristol raised the artifact, aiming it at Arthur, pressing the firing tab. Two seconds later he was gone.

Miss Bristol set the artifact down on the entryway table, taking a seat on a maroon velvet armchair, staring at the spot where Arthur had been standing. She leaned back in her chair, remembering the first time she had seen Arthur, when he was teaching a class on Mesoamerican pottery, how struck she had been by his kindness, by his encouragement, his enthusiasm.

She took out her phone, tapping on it, checking her email. There was one from Mrs. Smith, asking if Miss Bristol had thought any more about applying to Columbia University.

She replied to Mrs. Smith's email, saying she would apply once her social security number and identification cards were in hand, something which could take three or four more months.

She got to her feet, walking into the living room. It was a beautiful house, the perfect home for Arthur. He had been simultaneously living in 1910 and in 2025. She studied the lovely French paintings for a minute, then headed back to the entryway, taking a seat again, drumming her fingers on the arm of the chair. What if George was wrong? What if it didn't work? What if, what if, what if? Her thoughts were spiraling out of control. She did not want to think about such an unbearable possibility. She could hear the grandfather clock ticking in the hallway.

George had not been wrong.

Precisely sixteen minutes after Arthur vanished, there was a flash of brilliant light where he had been standing, a handsome young man appearing, dressed in an old man's suit. He groaned, staggering forward, pressing his hands to his head, leaning over.

Miss Bristol ran to him, helping him stand, holding him. "Arthur, your headache will be gone soon."

"I think I'm going to throw up, maybe faint. My head hurts."

"I know it does, you'll feel better soon, I promise." Miss Bristol set a plastic bucket on the floor in front of him. "Just in case you need it."

"Who are you? Where am I?"

"Your name is Arthur Hollingsworth, and I am Miss Bristol. You are safe here, this is your home. You have temporarily lost your memories, but I will stay with you, help you to get them back."

"Do I know you?"

"You do. You are the love of my life."

Epilogue

Arthur and Miss Bristol gazed up at The Temple of the Feathered Serpent, Arthur adjusting his wide-brimmed straw hat, sipping a glass of cold lemonade. "Excellent lemonade—the vendor said it was freshly squeezed."

Miss Bristol smiled. "You're sure you don't want to take the tour? It might be interesting to learn something about The Temple of the Feathered Serpent. Did you know he is also called Quetzalcoatl?"

"What an unusual name. I think I might have chosen a simpler one, something easier to spell."

"Something like Bob the Feathered Serpent?"

"It's almost as if you can read my mind."

"Shall we walk over to Beaumont's tunnel and see how time has treated it?"

Arthur said, "You will be pleased to know that nothing has changed in that regard since we were last here. Beaumont's tunnel has never been excavated, and it never will be, now that they have ceased all excavations. More tunnels and chambers have been discovered using ground-penetrating radar and ERT scans, but they are afraid any more excavations will destabilize the ground."

"So the two skeletons we found shall remain undisturbed for all eternity?"

"I should imagine it's for the best."

"Then we are of one mind."

A man carrying a wooden tray filled with colorful trinkets approached them with a broad smile. "I can see it in your eyes, the way you look at each other. You are on your honeymoon, you are newlyweds?"

Miss Bristol laughed. "You are quite correct, sir. Are you selling souvenirs of Teotihuacan?"

"They are a favorite of honeymooners, souvenirs to be cherished for years to come, a lasting symbol of your deep and eternal love for each other." The words flowed effortlessly from the vendor, as if he had said them a thousand times before.

Arthur picked up one of the colorful carved wooden figures, showing it to Miss Bristol. "What do you think?"

"It is Tláloc the Rain God, one of my favorites. We should get it."

"And what about this one, Xiuhcoatl the Fire Serpent?"

"Let's get them both, so we don't forget our time here at Teotihuacan."

The vendor was looking at them curiously. "You

know their names. This is most unusual."

Miss Bristol said, "We have studied Mesoamerican cultures in great depth, especially those of Teotihuacan. We are both anthropologists."

Arthur added, "We both hold degrees from Columbia University." He turned, smiling at Miss Bristol.

The vendor held up his hand. "Then they are yours, there is no charge. It pleases me that Tláloc and Xiuhcoatl shall live on in you."

"Are you sure?"

"I am sure." The vendor turned, heading toward another young couple, a broad smile on his face.

Arthur said, "That was nice of him. Why did you tell him we were newlyweds when we've been married for five years?"

"Time is relative, five years is the blink of an eye."

"Quite true."

Miss Bristol pulled her phone from her pocket, tapping it. "Good news, they found our reservations at the Gran Hotel Diligencias in Veracruz. We're all set for ten relaxing days at a most elegant luxury hotel, said to be the finest in Veracruz. I hope you brought your top hat and black tie. I've signed us up for a jungle tour while we're there. They said we'll see parrots."

"I've always wanted to see parrots, visit the Eiffel

Tower." He laughed.

Miss Bristol smiled. "You have quite an infectious laugh, sir."

"I'm glad we don't have to worry about Dr. Boas discovering how much money we're spending on a hotel."

"Somehow, wherever he is, I don't think Dr. Boas will mind. Did I tell you that Mrs. Smith called?"

"Is she all right?"

"She's fine. She wants to know if we would like George's collection of artifacts and his two albums of photographs. She also said she is going to pay Silas's college tuition. She has become quite good friends with Mrs. Wiggins, and Silas has been helping her take care of her house."

"I'm glad. It's nice of her to help Silas. I would love the artifacts and photo albums. We can set up a display in the sitting room. I'd love to see the pictures of you when you were young. I must say, you've aged quite nicely for someone born in 1885. You don't look a day over a hundred."

Miss Bristol laughed. "How kind of you to say so, dear Arthur. I owe my youthful appearance to exercise, plenty of rest, a healthy diet, and most of all, maintaining my eternal sense of wonder about the world we live in."

"I was wondering what your secret was, now I know."

"I think I have finally forgiven George for what he did."

"What changed your mind?"

"In looking at the grand picture, rather than just a single isolated incident, I came to realize that George unwittingly played a vital role in our eternal adventure."

"What do you mean?"

"Despite all the curious twists and turns and ups and downs that fate has set before us, including George's actions, here we are, you and I, together, back in Teotihuacan."

"Things always do seem to work out, don't they?"

"They do indeed, dear Arthur. We must hurry, the Tunnel Tour at the Pyramid of the Sun begins in thirty minutes. We don't want to miss it—they say it's quite thrilling."

"Perhaps we will see a scorpion."

"That would be thrilling. I'm getting shivers just thinking about it."

Arthur took Miss Bristol's hand, the two of them strolling down the Avenue of the Dead in the warm afternoon sun.

If you enjoyed reading

Miss Bristol Rents a Room

please leave a short review or rating
on Amazon.com
Reviews are the lifeblood of indie publishers –
we can't survive without them!

If you have any comments or suggestions
or would like to be notified of upcoming book
releases and Free Kindle book day promotions,
please email me at
OrvilleMouse@gmail.com

Follow me at:
www.facebook.com/TomHoffmanAuthor/

Best wishes until we meet again,

Tom Hoffman

ABOUT THE AUTHOR

Tom Hoffman received a B.S. in psychology from Georgetown University and a B.A. from the now-defunct Oregon College of Art. He has lived in Alaska with his wife since 1973. They have two adult children and four adorable grandchildren. Tom was a graphic designer and artist for over 35 years. Redirecting his imagination from art to writing, he wrote his first novel, The Eleventh Ring, at age 63

www.ingramcontent.com/pod-product-compliance
Lightning Source LLC
LaVergne TN
LVHW020534100826
845148LV00010B/1454
9798988405986